"I Want A Home..."

Leah felt Judd stiffen in her arms. "I'm thirty-nine, Judd. I don't have much more time. Surely you must know what a child would mean to me."

He pulled away from her, grasping her by the shoulders. With a wild, almost desperate look in his eyes, he gazed down at her. "I don't want to get married again, Leah, but if I ever do, I never want another child."

Searching his eyes for some sign of denial, Leah felt pinpricks of pain puncturing her heart. Surely he didn't mean what he'd said. The one thing on earth she wanted more than life itself was the one thing Judd Barnett said he never wanted....

Dear Reader:

Welcome to Silhouette Desire – provocative, compelling, contemporary love stories written by and for today's woman. These are stories to treasure.

Each and every Silhouette Desire is a wonderful romance in which the emotional and the sensual go hand in hand. When you open a Desire, you enter a whole new world – a world that has, naturally, a perfect hero just waiting to whisk you away! A Silhouette Desire can be light-hearted or serious, but it will always be satisfying.

We hope you enjoy this Desire today – and will go on to enjoy many more.

Please write to us:

Jane Nicholls
Silhouette Books
PO Box 236
Thornton Road
Croydon
Surrey
CR9 3RU

BEVERLY BARTON
THE WANDERER

Silhouette Desire

Originally Published by Silhouette Books
a division of
Harlequin Enterprises Ltd.

All the characters in this book have no existence outside the imagination of the Author, and have no relation whatsoever to anyone bearing the same name or names. They are not even distantly inspired by any individual known or unknown to the Author, and all the incidents are pure invention.

All rights reserved. The text of this publication or any part thereof may not be reproduced or transmitted in any form or by any means, electronic or mechanical, including photocopying, recording, storage in an information retrieval system, or otherwise, without the written permission of the publisher.

This book is sold subject to the condition that it shall not, by way of trade or otherwise, be lent, resold, hired out or otherwise circulated without the prior consent of the publisher in any form of binding or cover other than that in which it is published and without a similar condition including this condition being imposed on the subsequent purchaser.

*First published in Great Britain in 1993
by Silhouette Books, Eton House, 18-24 Paradise Road,
Richmond, Surrey TW9 1SR*

© Beverly Beaver 1993

*Silhouette, Silhouette Desire and Colophon are
Trade Marks of Harlequin Enterprises B.V.*

ISBN 0 373 58970 0

22-9307

Made and printed in Great Britain

To my editor, Wendy Corsi Staub, the very best.
We make a great team.
And to Lucia Macro, thanks for giving me so many
wonderful opportunities.

BEVERLY BARTON

has been in love with romance since her grandfather
gave her an illustrated book of *Beauty and the Beast*.
An avid reader since childhood, she began writing at the
age of nine, and wrote short stories, poetry, plays and
novels throughout school and college. After marriage to
her own "hero" and the births of her daughter and son,
she chose to be a full-time homemaker, a.k.a. wife,
mother, friend and volunteer.

Six years ago, she began substitute teaching and
returned to writing as a hobby. Her hobby became an
obsession as she devoted more and more time to improv-
ing her skills as a writer. Now, her lifelong dream of
being published has come true.

Other Silhouette Books by Beverly Barton

Silhouette Desire

Yankee Lover
Lucky in Love
Out of Danger
Sugar Hill
Talk of the Town

A Letter from the Author

Dear Reader:

I had seen him every day, and yet we hadn't shared a moment alone in weeks. The demands of our jobs and our family responsibilities had taken the romance out of our relationship. I wondered if he felt as neglected as I did.

Then one Saturday morning he asked me for a date. I could hardly believe it. My strong, silent-type husband of two decades, the man who considered me a hopeless romantic, had devised a plan for the two of us to share a whole day together. He even borrowed our daughter's red sports car for the event. The plan was simple and inexpensive, yet it's a day I'll treasure in my heart forever.

Late October in the South is a riot of color—everything golden with splashes of orange and red. As we drove along the Natchez Trace Parkway, the cruise control set on forty, we held hands and talked for endless hours. Making scenic stops along the way, we shared walks in the woods and by the Tennessee River. We became reacquainted as we traveled, as we absorbed the peace and beauty of autumn. We laughed, we talked, we kissed.

I learned anew that day what made Billy so special. Inside my old-fashioned macho man beat a gentle and caring heart—a heart that belonged to me. And so when we returned home before sunset, the two of us still holding hands, I knew something wonderful had happened on that special date—I felt as if I'd fallen in love all over again.

Sincerely,

Beverly Barton

Prologue

Only one limousine remained at Memphis Memorial Gardens. The long funeral procession had come and gone. Judd Barnett could not bring himself to leave. Although he had just buried his only child, not a tear fell from his hard, dark eyes. The pain inside him lay buried deep beneath the controlled emotions of a man who prided himself on his iron will. But he was having a difficult time handling the guilt that plagued him, the certain knowledge that he was responsible for his son's death.

Jared Barnett placed a comforting arm around his older brother's shoulder. "You shouldn't stay here any longer. There's nothing else you can do for Steven."

"There was damn little I did for him when he was alive." Judd looked down at the open grave, at the tiny casket that contained the lifeless body of his six-year-old son. Judd's chest ached with longing, with the need to go back and do it all over again, with the hopeless wish that he'd been a better father. Thankfully the numbness of unreality shielded Judd from the agony he knew was sure to come.

"You gave Steven everything," Jared said. "There wasn't anything he didn't have."

"Yeah, I bought him the best money could buy." Judd pulled away from his brother. "Steven had everything except his parents' time and attention."

"Don't do this to yourself. Carolyn isn't to blame and neither are you. It was an accident." Jared wiped the perspiration from his face with the palm of his hand.

"I should have sued for custody when we got the divorce. I knew how irresponsible Carolyn was." Judd turned from the graveside, his lean face a mask of calm. Even though the hot June breeze did nothing to cool his suit-clad body, Judd barely felt the heat. "But I was too busy building an empire to have time for my son."

"Southland Inns would have belonged to Steven someday. You were building an empire for him."

"The hell I was," Judd said as he walked toward the limousine. "I did it for myself. Money and power is all that matters. Isn't that what the old man taught us? If you can't buy it, it's not worth having."

Jared followed, slipping inside the back of the limo beside his brother. "You'll get married again one of these days. You'll have other children. My God, you're only thirty-seven."

"I don't ever want another child." Judd motioned to the chauffeur. "And I don't want my empire anymore."

"What are you saying?"

"I'm saying that as soon as I can make arrangements for you to take over Southland Inns, I'm leaving."

"Where are you going, and for how long?"

"I don't know," Judd said. "A few months, a few years, the rest of my life."

One

"**I** certainly wouldn't want Stanley Woolton to father my child," Myrtle Mae Derryberry said, turning sharply to face her niece who was driving through late-evening traffic.

"I thought I told you that I didn't want to discuss this anymore." Leah clutched the steering wheel of her twelve-year-old Chevrolet station wagon. She'd had a long, busy day at the shop. Now, the beginnings of a sick headache plagued her, and Aunt Myrt's endless prattle about Stanley wasn't helping any.

"Well, I'm not through discussing it." Myrt tilted her head slightly, bouncing the ends of her bright red hair against her plump shoulder. "I realize that you're going through some sort of mid-life crisis just because you're facing your thirty-ninth birthday single and childless. But that's no reason to consider marrying a nerd like Stanley."

"Stanley isn't a nerd. He's a very successful accountant." Leah turned off the main thoroughfare onto a side street that led to Hamburger Heaven. Takeouts would have

10 THE WANDERER

to suffice for supper; she certainly didn't feel up to cooking. "Besides, we're only dating. Marriage hasn't even come up. Yet."

"Yet?"

Myrt's voice had a deep, gravelly quality that, she had told Leah on more than one occasion, turned men on. Leah knew her own voice had that same sultry sound, but she didn't think either she or her voice had ever really turned on any man. "Can we please postpone this discussion until a later time?"

"You've always been a bit of a prude, Leah, sweetie, but surely you want more than lukewarm affection. I realize you've never had a grand passion, but, believe me, once you've been madly in love, you'd never settle for anything less."

Leah maneuvered the station wagon through the underpass. In her peripheral vision, she noticed a small band of vagrants huddled around a fire burning inside a large metal drum. The orange flames licked upward into the night sky, illuminating the shadowy silhouettes of several men.

"All I want is marriage to a nice man and a child of my own before I'm too old to have children. Surely, Aunt Myrt, you can understand. You've told me, many times, how much you regret not having children."

"You're my child, or at least the next best thing." Myrt laughed, the warm, unrestrained sound filling the inside of the vehicle. "And I didn't have to bed a man I didn't love to get you."

Despite her throbbing head and her irritation at Aunt Myrt, Leah couldn't refrain from laughing, too. Her aunt had always had a way of making Leah see the humorous side of things. Sometimes she envied her mother's sister the ability to live life so freely and unrestrained.

"Well, unless I fall madly, passionately in love soon, I'm not going to keep waiting for Prince Charming to show up. I've been waiting for years," Leah said.

THE WANDERER

"You've been raising your brother and sister and taking care of one slightly eccentric aunt since you were twenty-one. Your responsibilities to us kept you from—"

A thumping bang vibrated through the car; a series of bumps announced trouble. Leah pulled off the side of the road near the underpass.

"What on earth's the matter?" Myrt asked.

"I think we've had a flat tire," Leah said as she killed the motor. "You stay inside where it's warm and I'll check the tires. It felt like the right front was pulling."

Before Myrt could reply, Leah opened the door, stepped out and walked around the front of the station wagon. She groaned when she saw the deflated condition of the tire. This is all I need, she thought. Since Pattie had been sick, she'd had to handle the shop all day by herself. A new shipment of Yankee candles had arrived, and a third had been broken. And Stanley's mother, Cora, had persuaded Leah to be on the committee for the upcoming charity ball at the country club. Something she definitely didn't have the time to do. And ever since Aunt Myrt had stopped by the shop at three, Leah had been listening to a constant sermon on marriage, children and love. Now, this. The flat tire was definitely the last straw.

Without thinking, Leah kicked the tire with all her might. She felt the jarring pain shoot through her foot and radiate up her leg. She wanted to curse, but well-bred southern ladies didn't curse. She wanted to cry, but strong southern women didn't cry over flat tires.

"Well, it's certainly flat, isn't it?" Myrt said, then like a playful child blew her breath into the cold night air and watched the smoky results with total fascination.

Leah jumped, jerking her hands up in front of her face and clenching her fists. "Goodness, Aunt Myrt, you scared me to death. I thought I told you to stay inside the car."

"I decided I would be of more help out here."

12   THE WANDERER

"Please get back in." Leah walked toward the back of the wagon. "I've got a spare tire. I just hope I remember the way Larry showed me how to change it."

"You can't mean that you intend to try to change the tire yourself!" With mouth agape and eyes wide, Myrt stared at her niece. "Just because your brother showed you how doesn't mean he actually thought you'd ever do it."

Leah opened the tailgate. "Do you have another suggestion? The nearest service station is at least two miles from here."

"Hamburger Heaven is less than a mile, and they do have a phone," Myrt said. "Of course, I believe there's an easier solution. Just wait here."

Leah watched, uncertain what her aunt had in mind. Then when she realized Myrt was headed straight toward the small group of vagrants warming themselves around the fire, Leah made a mad dash to stop her.

"Aunt Myrt!"

"Gentlemen, it seems my niece and I have a little problem." Myrt smiled that million-dollar smile that had charmed numerous men. "We desperately need one of you big, strong men to change our flat tire."

Oh, God, please don't let this be happening, Leah thought. These men could be rapists and killers at worst, thieves and lazy bums at best.

A tall, robust man with a mane of silver hair stepped out of the small gathering. He wore dark, faded pants and a heavy woolen coat, patched in several places. An old felt hat sat tilted on his head.

"Yes, ma'am." His voice was deep, midwestern accented and surprisingly cultured. "My friend and I..." He reached out and took another man by the arm, tugging slightly. The other vagrant turned around. "We'll be glad to take care of your problem, won't we, Judd?"

Leah stood, frozen to the spot. She simply didn't know how to handle the situation. If she rushed forward, grabbed Aunt Myrt and declined the man's offer, what would hap-

THE WANDERER 13

pen? Would these men attack? Surely they intended to ask
to be paid for fixing the flat and might be upset if Leah de-
nied them the chance to make some money. On the other
hand, perhaps they were just good-hearted men down on
their luck and were willing to do a good deed in exchange for
enough money to pay for a meal.

The man called Judd eyed his friend, but Leah couldn't
make out the look on his face. The only illumination came
from the station wagon's headlights, the blazing fire and a
lone streetlight several yards away. Without saying a word,
Judd jerked away from the other man and walked toward
Leah. She noticed that Aunt Myrt had struck up a conversation with the older gentleman.

When the one named Judd approached Leah, she saw
that he was extremely tall. Probably six foot four. And he
was big... really big. His shoulders seemed enormous inside the tattered old leather jacket he wore, and his long legs
were heavy with muscles. Realizing she was inspecting his
body, Leah moved her gaze upward, encountering his face,
which was covered with a thick beard. His dark auburn hair
was overly long and curled about his ears.

"Show me where the jack and the extra are," he said.

"I...er...in the back of the wagon," she finally managed to reply. Leah couldn't ever remember being so overwhelmed by a man—by his size, his physique, the sad, lonely
look in his eyes. Brown eyes. Cinnamon-brown eyes.

Without giving her a second glance, Judd headed toward
the rear of the Chevy. Taking several deep breaths, Leah
regained her composure and followed.

"I...we certainly do appreciate this," she said. "I'm
afraid I've never changed a flat before."

"Yeah." He reached inside the wagon, removed the jack
and lug wrench, then carried them to the front of the car.

Leah watched, fascinated by how adeptly he placed the
jack under the front bumper. Strange, she thought, how
men seemed to have a knack for such things. Then of
course, she knew if Pattie had been along, she would have

14 THE WANDERER

known exactly what to do. Her friend and employee, Pattie Cornell, considered herself a modern woman, capable of taking care of herself without any help from the male sex. Leah admitted that she herself was a bit more old-fashioned.

"Is there anything I can do to help?" she asked, smiling. The unfriendly look on Judd's face erased the smile from hers.

"Just stay out of the way. Okay?" Judd didn't mind helping ladies in distress. What he objected to was the way this one made him feel. He'd taken one look into her big blue eyes and wondered what she'd be like in bed. He couldn't remember the last time he'd been instantly attracted to a woman, and his common sense told him that he'd better steer clear of trouble.

"Do you need your friend?" Leah nodded toward the older man who stood several feet away, obviously enjoying a lighthearted conversation with Myrt. Both of them were laughing. Surely her aunt wouldn't embarrass her further by flirting with some dirty, shiftless bum. But Leah knew better. Myrtle Mae Derryberry was known for doing the unthinkable.

"I don't need him," Judd assured her as he inserted the beveled end of the lug wrench beneath the hubcap and popped it off. "Besides, I think Taylor is otherwise occupied."

Leah hated to agree, but it was apparent that neither her aunt nor the man named Taylor was the least bit interested in the flat tire. "Are you and Mr. Taylor from Marshallton?"

Judd laid the hubcap on the ground, then loosened the lug nuts. "Look, I know Taylor and I make you uncomfortable, so there's no need for you to try to make polite conversation." Judd's instincts warned him against being friendly. In a day or two he'd be moving on. He didn't want this woman becoming a reason for him to stay.

Leah started to assure him that he was mistaken, but thought better of the idea when he gave her a distinctly

THE WANDERER

chilling stare. She glanced over at Aunt Myrt, who had placed her hand on Taylor's arm and seemed to be whispering something to him. When the man took Myrt's hand in his, Leah moved forward, then stopped herself.

"If you're worried about your mother, then go over there and tell Taylor to leave her alone." Judd could see that she didn't approve of what was going on, that, like most people, she considered homeless men to be dirty, lazy and probably dangerous. Of course, she had every right to be nervous. Smart women didn't take unnecessary risks where strange men were concerned.

"She's my aunt."

Judd walked around to the front of the station wagon and finished jacking up the car until the wheel cleared the ground. "I understand why you're wary of us, but there's really no need to be. Neither of us are killers or thieves." He glanced up at her and grinned. "And, honey, I wouldn't jump your bones without an invitation."

With his back to her, Judd couldn't help smiling when he heard her sharp intake of breath. No doubt, he had insulted her. That had been his intention. He couldn't take the chance that she might like him.

"That remark was totally uncalled for," Leah said as she took a step closer, her legs only inches from his hip where he squatted beside the front fender.

Judd removed the loose lug nuts, laid them inside the hubcap, then pulled off the wheel. "Leave me alone, lady. In a few minutes, I'll have this job finished and you and your aunt can be on your way."

Leah followed him when he picked up the flat tire and carried it around to the back of the wagon. Goodness, he's awfully strong, she thought. Big and strong and all man. There was something about him . . . some strange magnetic appeal that fascinated Leah. "I . . . I appreciate your doing this for us. It was . . . kind of you."

Judd dumped the tire into the wagon bed, pulled out the spare and rolled it forward. "I'm a lot of things, lady, but kind isn't one of them."

Leah could feel the color seep into her face, and thanked the Lord that it was too dark for Judd to notice. He was, without a doubt, one of the rudest men she'd ever met. She didn't reply. What could she say? Standing silently, she watched while he replaced the tire, his big, strong hands moving swiftly and with consummate accuracy. She couldn't keep herself from staring at him, surprised that she found a bearded, long-haired, disheveled-looking man so attractive. There was something so...so male about him.

"Finished," Judd said, standing up with the jack and lug wrench in his hand.

He made a thorough inspection of her. She wasn't bad-looking, what he could see of her in her tan coat and brown suede boots. Her clothing reflected neither wealth nor current style, but rather a sedate sense of good breeding. She was pretty, but she appeared rather severe and spinsterish with her dark hair pulled back into a loose bun. Her attitude said it all. Her entire manner was one of cool superiority. It was obvious she considered him beneath her. So why the hell did he want her when he hadn't really wanted a woman in years? "Oh, yes. Thank you." Leah opened her purse, scrambling around inside to find her wallet. She pulled out a ten-dollar bill and handed it to him.

He looked down at the money, then up at her. When he reached out, Leah noticed that his hands were fairly clean, his nails neatly trimmed. His clothes were old and worn, but he wasn't dirty. He smelled of cold, fresh air and masculine warmth.

"We can't take the lady's money, can we, Judd?" Taylor said, coming up beside his friend.

Leah looked at the two men. Aunt Myrt's arm was draped over Taylor's. They appeared to be a couple out for a nightly stroll. "Of course you can," Leah said. "I insist."

THE WANDERER

"I have a much better idea," Myrt said. "If Taylor and Judd are too gentlemanly to accept money, then perhaps they'll agree to join us for supper."

"What?" The words came from Leah's throat in a keen squeal.

"We can't do that," Judd said.

But Leah knew it was already too late. Taylor had opened the car door for Aunt Myrt, who was getting inside. Within seconds Taylor followed her, slamming the door. The older couple sat there looking like two teenagers in the back seat at a drive-in theater.

"Looks like we've been outvoted." Judd didn't want to go anywhere with this woman. She might try to hide the fact, but it was clear to him that she was a bit of a snob. A damned good-looking snob, but a snob all the same. And the longer he was around her, the more he'd want her. Something told him that this lady was the type who played for keeps. He was a drifter, a wanderer. The last thing he wanted was permanent ties of any kind. Despite the fact that he hadn't eaten since yesterday, he'd rather take her ten bucks than share a meal with her.

"We're just going up the road a piece to Hamburger Heaven," Leah told him.

"I like hamburgers." Somebody should kick his back end. Why had he said that? He should be talking himself out of this dinner offer, shouldn't he?

"Yes ... well ... I suppose we should be going."

He reached out, grabbing her by the wrist. Leah spun around, facing him, surprise and fear in her eyes.

"Look, lady, Taylor and I are harmless. We aren't going to hurt you and your aunt. We're just a couple of guys down on our luck."

"I see."

"You have every right not to trust us." He ran his thumb over the pulse point in her wrist. "If you want me to, I'll get Taylor out of the car, but your aunt doesn't seem to have any doubts about him."

"My aunt comes from another generation. A less-wary generation." Leah tried to pull away from Judd, but he held her wrist tightly.

"My name is Judd Barnett."

Leah looked at him, really looked at him. Brown eyes met blue eyes. She wondered what he looked like beneath all that hair. Was he handsome? His eyes were beautiful. Dark rich brown, framed by thick copper lashes. His nose was long and straight and his cheekbones high and sharp.

"I'm Leah Marshall, Mr. Barnett. You can sit in the front seat with me."

"Are you sure you want to do this?"

"No, I'm not sure, but Aunt Myrt seems determined, and despite the fact that people think she's crazy, she's a pretty good judge of character."

"What about you, Leah Marshall, are you easily fooled?"

"No more and no less than the next person." She didn't know how much longer she'd be able to bear his touch. The feel of his huge hand wrapped around her wrist was doing strange things to her insides. Her stomach was doing flip-flops, and she felt hot and cold all at the same time.

Taylor rolled down the window. "What's keeping you two? Myrtle Mae and I are dying of starvation."

"Let's go," Leah said, jerking her hand out of Judd's grasp.

Plastic ferns, placed strategically away from the ceiling fans, hung from the rafters. Old photographs of Marshallton's early days decorated the walls. A multicolored jukebox stood against the back wall; a medley of fifties and sixties classics added what the owners of Hamburger Heaven considered nostalgic atmosphere. The Drifters's "Save the Last Dance for Me" had just ended, and Myrt and Taylor were discussing the possibility of finding an uncluttered floor area where they could dance. Judd recognized the look of panic on Leah's face. Undoubtedly her

THE WANDERER 19

aunt's behavior had proved an embarrassment to the rather straitlaced Ms. Marshall on more than one occasion.

Judd finished off the last bite of his second hamburger, then downed the remainder of his third cup of coffee. He hadn't realized how hungry he was until they'd stepped inside the burger joint and he'd smelled the delicious, greasy aroma of French fries.

"It's not very crowded in here tonight," Myrt said. "Of course it's the middle of the week."

"Do you and your niece eat here often?" Taylor asked.

"Occasionally, when Leah's had a difficult day and doesn't feel up to cooking supper," Myrt said.

"You don't cook, Ms. Derryberry?" Judd asked.

"It's a disgrace, isn't it, a woman my age who can't cook?" Myrt shook her head sadly. "I've just never been the domestic type. I ran off and led a gypsy life for years. That's when I found out that there are other things just as important to men as food."

"Aunt Myrt!" Leah scolded, but her tone was whisper-soft. She glanced around to see if any of the other patrons had overheard her aunt's comment.

"Oh, hush, Leah." Myrt glanced at Judd, then at Taylor and winked. "I'm right, aren't I, gentlemen? The male species does have other appetites just as strong as their lust for home-cooked meals, don't they?"

Judd twisted his mouth, trying not to smile. He grunted, then coughed and finally managed to control the laughter bubbling just beneath the surface. Obviously Myrtle Mae knew a lot more about men than her niece did.

"Right you are, Myrtle Mae, my love," Taylor said. "Man, indeed, does not live by bread alone."

Myrt smiled at Taylor as she laid her hand over his where it rested on the table. "There's not a soul sitting at those tables back there. We could push them over a little and make enough room to dance."

Taylor inspected the area in question. "I do believe you're right."

20   THE WANDERER

When Taylor and Myrt stood, Leah reached out, trying to grab her aunt's hand. "Aunt Myrt! Please..."

Myrt patted Leah on the shoulder. "Now, you just go ahead and have a nice little chat with Judd here. Taylor and I aren't going to get into any trouble. We'll just be right back there."

"But, Aunt Myrt—"

"Hush, now. Why don't you two order hot-fudge sundaes?" Completely ignoring Leah, Myrt took Taylor's hand.

"Aunt Myrt, people don't dance in here. You're going to make a spectacle of yourself." When Leah saw that her aunt was ignoring her, she leaned over, covering her face with her hands and sighing deeply. Her head throbbed. Closing her eyes, she rubbed her temples in a circular motion and prayed that when she opened her eyes, she would find herself at home, alone.

"I'd like a hot-fudge sundae," Judd said.

Leah snapped her head around, focusing on the man sitting beside her. "What?"

"Leave them alone. Let them have a little fun." Judd nodded toward the older couple who were busy rearranging several tables and chairs at the back of the restaurant. "What difference does it make if a few people in here watch them, and maybe even laugh at them?"

"You don't have to live in this town, Mr. Barnett," Leah said. "I do."

"So?" Judd hailed the waitress who quickly made her way over to their booth.

"I have a business in Marshallton, a social position and a reputation to uphold, and furthermore—"

"Take your order, sir?" The young, skinny waitress was chewing gum at a speed that could break the sound barrier.

"Two hot-fudge sundaes," Judd said.

"Coming right up." The girl glanced toward the back of the room, then laughed. "Look at those two, would you?

THE WANDERER

They're old enough to be my grandparents and they're back there dancing. Aren't they cute?''

"I don't want a hot-fudge sundae." Leah also didn't want to lose her temper, but she was fast losing patience not only with Judd and Myrt and Taylor, but with the whole situation. When she'd left work today, all she'd wanted was a quick hamburger, a hot bath and a good night's sleep. Instead she had walked right into a nightmare, and an unwanted attraction for a man she didn't even know.

"You'll want it when it gets here." Judd turned around and looked over his shoulder. Mary Wells's "My Guy" was playing on the jukebox. Myrt and Taylor cuddled close, Taylor's right hand resting possessively on his partner's plump hip. "Which is it that you're so opposed to, Ms. Marshall, romance or sex?"

"I beg your pardon?" Leah wasn't sure she'd heard him correctly. Had this man, this bum she'd picked up on the side of the road and fed, taunted her about sex? Surely not.

"It seems to bother you that your aunt and Taylor are attracted to each other."

"That's ridiculous. They don't even know each other. They just met."

"Then you don't believe in love at first sight?" Hell, he didn't believe in love of any kind, but he certainly did believe in lust, and right now he was being bombarded with a double dose of that old animalistic urge. Judd surrounded his empty foam coffee cup with both hands, crushing it.

Leah jumped at the crackling sound of the cup smashing beneath Judd's strong fingers. Flinging her right hand up to her forehead, she massaged her temple. The pounding in her head intensified. "Look, Mr. Barnett, I had a difficult day at work, a flat tire that I'm grateful you fixed and now a splitting headache. Add to that the fact that my already-notorious aunt is making a spectacle of herself with some...some man we don't even know—"

Judd held up both his big hands in front of him in a signal for Leah to stop. "I get the message. Believe me, I got it the minute we met." It was apparent that Leah Marshall had taken one look at him and dismissed him. He was a peasant to her princess, a servant to her lady of the manor. The intense attraction he felt was a one-sided affliction. She just plain wasn't interested, and he should consider himself lucky.

"If for one minute you're implying that I'm attracted to you—"

Before she could finish the sentence, Judd roared with laughter. Well, I'll be damned, he thought, Miss Uptight Too-good-for-the-likes-of-you *was* as attracted to him as her aunt was to Taylor. And all the while he had assumed that her animosity was snobbery. Instead she was angry with herself for being attracted to a bum. Now what was he going to do? "Obviously you object to romance and sex for yourself as well as Myrtle Mae."

"I have no objections to romance...or...or to sex for that matter, but I do have an objection to—"

"Here we go folks, two hot-fudge sundaes." The waitress set their chocolate-covered ice cream desserts down on the table in front of them. "Did you notice that some of the kids have started dancing with the old folks?"

Leah looked toward the back of the restaurant where two teenage couples had joined Myrt and Taylor, swaying in one another's arms to the rhythm of Percy Sledge's "When a Man Loves a Woman." Leah glanced up at the waitress who had already turned to take the orders at another table. Despite the fact that she knew it would be a mistake to look at Judd, she couldn't stop herself. He was staring at her, the smile on his face gone, replaced by an intense glare.

As the heavy beat of drums echoed through Hamburger Heaven, Leah watched Judd Barnett, captured by the loneliness and passion she saw so clearly in his whiskey-brown eyes. And Judd watched Leah Marshall, deeply disturbed by the desire inside him, the primitive longing he hadn't felt in years. Why now? he asked the powers that be. And why

THE WANDERER

her? A repressed little snob who obviously hated being attracted to a man she considered to be no more than scum.

As the music continued and the rough sounds of the singer's bluesy voice shouted out the message about a man's basic need for his woman, Leah felt a spreading warmth seep through every inch of her body. Dear Lord, what was happening to her? She had never experienced anything like this. And it was all Judd Barnett's fault. He was looking at her as if...as if—

"Well, hello, Ms. Marshall. What are you and your aunt doing here at Hamburger Heaven tonight?" The voice belonged to a handsome teenage boy standing at the side of the table.

Leah jerked her gaze away from Judd and looked up directly into the condemning hazel eyes of Stanley Woolton III. "Ah...er...hello, Trey." Why, of all people in Marshallton, did Stanley's son have to be the one to catch her and Aunt Myrt *entertaining* a couple of shoddily dressed bums? And Aunt Myrt was dancing with one of them, causing a public spectacle of herself. Leah wished she could crawl under the table and hide.

"I don't believe we've met," Trey said, offering his hand to Judd. "I'm Trey Woolton. My father is one of Ms. Marshall's oldest and dearest friends."

Judd glanced at the boy's immaculately manicured hand. A soft, pretty hand. Almost effeminate. Judd grasped the hand more tightly than was necessary, smiling to himself when he saw the grimace on the young man's face. "I'm Judd Barnett, Ms. Marshall's dinner companion for the evening."

Trey laughed, a sound somewhere between a giggle and a snicker. "Double date?" he asked, nodding toward the back of the restaurant where Myrt and Taylor had stopped dancing and were walking toward them.

"Please give your father and grandmother my best." Leah hoped that Trey would leave before Myrt got a chance to speak to him. Her aunt had made it perfectly clear that she disliked Stanley's son more than she did Stanley. She thought he was a troublemaker.

"Well, if it isn't little Trey," Myrt called out from several yards away. "Don't tell me that Cora Woolton let you out on a school night. Lord knows what the world is coming to when teenagers are allowed to eat hamburgers and dance to oldies when they should be home preparing themselves for their ACT tests."

Leah groaned silently, longing for a convenient escape, but none seemed forthcoming. "We really should be going. If you don't mind—"

"We haven't eaten our sundaes, and the ice cream is melting fast," Judd said, smiling at Leah, knowing full well that she was utterly embarrassed by the situation.

"I don't want mine." She flashed Judd a phony smile. "Feel free to finish yours, but Aunt Myrt and I—"

"Don't forget to pay the bill." Judd picked up the slip of paper from the table and held it out to Leah who had already stood and was trying to slip into her coat.

She snatched the bill out of his hand. "Thank you, gentlemen, for your assistance tonight." She nodded at Taylor and gave Judd a warning glare. "Good night, Trey."

"I'll see you ladies to your car," Taylor said, tightening his hold on Myrt's arm.

"There's no need. Honestly," Leah said.

"I insist." Taylor escorted Myrt toward the door.

Leah followed them outside, not once looking back at either Judd or Trey Woolton.

"Now, Taylor," Myrt said, "don't forget to come by the house tomorrow and I'll help you line up some odd jobs. I know several people who still need some yard work done, and then there's—"

"Are you staying here in Marshallton, Mr. Taylor?" Leah asked, despite the fact that interrupting her aunt had shown a sad lack of good manners.

"Oh, yes, now that I've met Myrtle Mae, I intend to stay on indefinitely." Taylor gazed down into Myrt's green eyes

THE WANDERER

as he took her hand, brought it to his lips and pressed several delicate kisses across her knuckles.

"Isn't it wonderful, Leah?" Myrt gave Taylor a loving pat on his stubble-covered cheek. "Having that flat tire tonight was fate. It brought two handsome men into our lives."

Leah took a deep breath. *Stay calm,* she told herself. *Just get Aunt Myrt in the car, and you can deal with this ridiculous situation later.* "We really should be going."

"Aren't you going to say goodbye to Judd?" Myrt asked.

"We've already said goodbye." Leah prayed that she'd never see Judd Barnett again. The man did strange things to her nerves.

"The hot-fudge sundae was delicious," Judd said walking up behind Leah. "You should have stayed and eaten yours." He surveyed her from the top of her dark brown hair to the tips of her suede boots. "Of course, you're probably watching your weight."

Leah froze to the spot. How on earth had the man eaten his sundae so quickly? He must have devoured it. And how dare he imply that she was overweight. No doubt he was referring to her hips. She'd always had broad hips.

Leah tugged on Myrt's arm, freeing her from Taylor's hold. "Well, gentlemen, good night and goodbye."

She tried unsuccessfully to gently shove Myrt into the front seat of the station wagon. Myrt bucked. "Just a minute. I almost forgot to tell Judd something."

"What?" Leah and Judd uttered the question simultaneously.

"I know where you can find a job, too." Myrt's lips curved into a deviously triumphant smile. "Leah always hires a handyman-deliveryman this time of year. You go by her shop in the morning and she'll put you to work, won't you, Leah?"

"I...I usually hire a teenager or a retired gentleman—" Leah balked at the very idea of Judd Barnett working for her.

26   THE WANDERER

"So, this year you'll hire a big, strong man in his prime. After all, Judd desperately needs the work, don't you, Judd?" Myrt turned her glowing smile on the man in question.

"Where is your shop?" Judd asked, giving his full attention to Leah.

"Downtown. Country Class. You can't miss it." With that said, Leah nudged Myrt inside the station wagon, rushed around to the driver's side and gave Judd and Taylor a quick wave. Once inside, she slammed the door, inserted the ignition key and revved the motor. Before Myrt could get her window rolled down to say anything more, Leah zoomed out of the parking lot so quickly she almost collided with an incoming truck.

"My heavens, you certainly are in a hurry." Myrt struggled to secure her seat belt.

Once she had maneuvered the wagon onto the main thoroughfare, Leah glanced over at her aunt. "You shouldn't have encouraged that man."

"I wanted to encourage Taylor. I like him. I like him a lot. And he likes me."

"I wasn't referring to *your* Mr. Taylor, although I absolutely forbid you to have anything else to do with that man. I was speaking of Judd Barnett."

"You can't forbid me to see Taylor," Myrt said. "Why are you acting so strangely, Leah? Are you ill?"

"No. Yes! I'm sick to death of your irrational behavior. I'm constantly having to defend you to my friends, my customers, my business associates and to—"

"To Stanley Woolton and that heifer of a mother of his?" Myrt sat up straight, ran her fingers through her hair and tilted her head, sticking her nose haughtily into the air. "We don't have to defend ourselves to the Wooltons. After all, least you forget, Leah, my sweet, we are Derryberrys. Your great-great-grandfather James Clayburn Derryberry was a colonel in the Confederate army, and Cora Woolton's fam-

THE WANDERER

ily didn't even come south until reconstruction. Carpetbaggers. The whole lot of them.''

''Aunt Myrt, don't start—''

''And your illustrious ancestor John Herston Marshall founded this town.''

''Our family history has nothing to do with the fact that you offered some worthless tramp a job at my store. He's nothing but a wanderer. We don't know anything about the man, except—''

''Except that he's handsome and extremely sexy.'' Myrt sighed.

''I was going to say that he was rude and showed a disgraceful lack of manners,'' Leah said.

''Well, I'll tell you one thing, if I were looking for a man to give me a baby, I'd be figuring out a way to seduce Judd Barnett. He sure as hell would make the whole process more exciting and enjoyable than Stanley Woolton ever could.''

Only by the grace of God did Leah keep from wrecking the station wagon. As quickly as she lost control of both the vehicle and her temper, she regained her senses and managed to keep the wagon from swerving into a nearby ditch. She wasn't sure what upset her more, the insanity of her aunt's suggestion or the momentary thought of what it would be like to make love with Judd Barnett.

Two

Leah checked her watch for the tenth time in the last hour. It was eleven-forty-five, and Judd Barnett hadn't shown up. She told herself that she should be relieved, that he probably wasn't even in town anymore, but some insistent little voice inside her kept telling her that she was disappointed.

As she flicked the feather duster across the wicker doll furniture in the display window, Leah mumbled to herself. "I was not the least bit attracted to that man. I do not want to see him again. Okay, so I dreamed about him last night. No big deal. A woman has no control over her dreams."

"Who are you talking to?" Pattie Cornell asked, walking out of the downstairs storeroom.

Leah jumped, then gasped. "Nobody. Just giving myself a little lecture."

"What's the matter with you? You've been nervous all morning. Are you afraid Stanley's going to make an unexpected visit, get down on one knee to propose, and you won't be able to think of a diplomatic way to refuse him?"

THE WANDERER 29

Pattie, her big brown eyes twinkling with mischievousness, smiled at her employer.

Leah straightened the hand-crocheted afghan on display before turning around. "I don't know who's the worst, you, Aunt Myrt or Larry. I can't understand why you're all so totally opposed to my dating Stanley."

"We don't care if you date Stanley. We just don't want you to marry the little weasel."

"He's not a weasel!"

"Who's not a weasel?" Milly Wilson asked when she entered the shop, holding a baby on her hip and clutching a toddler's hand.

"Stanley Woolton," Pattie said, rolling her eyes heavenward just in time to avoid seeing Leah's scowling expression.

"I wouldn't go so far as to call him a weasel, but...Leah, surely you aren't still considering marrying him, are you?" Milly asked just as her toddler broke free. "Come back here right this minute."

Pattie scooped Milly's two-year-old son up in her arms. "Just look at Todd. Isn't he beautiful? You can't have a child who looks like this if he's fathered by a man like Stanley."

"Trey is a very handsome boy," Leah reminded her friend.

"Well, he looks a lot like his mother did," Pattie said. "Besides, people have wondered for years if—"

"Don't say it." Leah gave her friend and employee a warning stare.

"What can we do for you today, Milly?" Pattie asked, turning her attention to their customer. "Are you doing some Christmas shopping?"

"No. Eric's parents have an anniversary coming up and his mother collects depression glass. The red depression glass."

"We've got several nice pieces in one of the back cases."
When Leah started toward the back of the shop, Milly and
baby following, the front door opened.

Leah swallowed hard. Judd Barnett, all six feet four
inches of him, stood just inside the doorway. Three women
stared at him.

"My, my, my," Pattie said.

"Wow!" Milly whispered, but she might as well have
shouted. The expression on her face said it all.

Quickly pulling herself out of her mental trance, Leah
turned around to fully face Judd. With a wave of her hand
to Pattie, she motioned her employee to her. "Pattie, will
you show Milly the red depression glass? I'll take care of this
gentleman."

"Lucky you," Pattie said, then eased Todd downward
onto his feet. After inspecting the four adults in the room,
the child made a mad dash toward his mother.

Clutching the fingers of her left hand over the back side
of her folded right hand, Leah marched forward. She tried
to smile, but the closer she got to Judd, the louder her heart
pounded and the more her stomach churned.

"Hello," she said, extending her hand. Judd accepted her
hand, but instead of exchanging a quick, casual shake, he
held tightly. He wasn't sure whether or not she was glad to
see him. She acted friendly enough, but he suspected that
was for the benefit of the others present. More than likely
she had hoped she'd never see him again. Hell, he was
probably a fool for showing up, for actually wanting to see
her badly enough to consider taking the job and sticking
around Marshallton for a while.

"Is the job offer still open?" he asked.

Leah nodded affirmatively, then pulled on her hand. He
held fast. She looked at him pleadingly as she gave Pattie
and Milly a sidelong glance. "Why don't you come into my
office, Mr. Barnett?"

THE WANDERER 31

"Yeah. Okay." Following her toward the back of the store, he acknowledged the stares of the other women with a polite nod.

Leah heard Milly's giggle and Pattie's soft whistle when Judd passed them. Leah turned sharply, giving Pattie a condemning glare. "You'll have to excuse my friends, Mr. Barnett. Obviously, they've never seen a man before."

Judd smiled. First at Leah, and then at Pattie and Milly. Todd, who'd been busying himself pulling place mats off a nearby shelf, stopped and looked up at Judd. Picking up a wooden napkin ring, the child walked toward the big man who had just noticed him.

"Ring, Daddy, ring," Todd said, offering Judd the small round object he held in his hand.

Judd froze to the spot at the sound of the child's voice. The little boy had big brown eyes and reddish-blond curls. Steven. The toddler looked like Steven had at that age. Judd felt an overwhelming desire to reach out and take the child in his arms, but he didn't. This child wasn't his. His son was dead. He'd been dead for over three years.

Leah noticed the strange play of emotions crossing Judd's face, and was puzzled by the intense way he stared at Todd. There was something wrong, terribly wrong.

"Todd calls all men daddy," Leah said.

Milly came up behind her son, lifting him into her arms. "The man doesn't want to see your ring right now, sweetheart. Come show it to Pattie."

"My office is back this way." Leah walked over to Judd, taking him by the arm. His arm was rock hard, not just from sheer muscular strength, but from rigid control. For some reason, Todd's innocent greeting had affected Judd in an odd way. Did he dislike children? Leah wondered.

Judd hated himself for still feeling so much pain and guilt over Steven's death. After all these years he couldn't stop running, trying to escape the memories that haunted him no matter where he went. How could a man ever come to terms

32 THE WANDERER

with the death of his child when he knew he was responsible?

"Judd? Are you all right?" Leah tugged on his arm.

He looked at her and saw concern in her eyes. Deep blue eyes filled with compassion and gentleness. "Yeah. Fine."

He followed her into her office, taking note only of the pale green and pink colors that dominated the small room and how femininely it was decorated.

"Sit down, please." She pointed to a wing-back Queen Anne chair placed against the wall across from her desk.

"Look, like I told you last night, there's no need for—"

"I'm trying my level best to remember my manners, Mr. Barnett." Leah spread out her hand, motioning again for him to be seated. "As you may recall, it wasn't my idea to ask you to fix my tire, share my evening meal or offer you a job."

"Your Aunt Myrtle is quite a woman, isn't she?" Judd sat. He couldn't remember the last time a woman had interested him so much. And he didn't mean Myrtle Mae. Leah Marshall was something. He had an idea that underneath all her southern manners and ladylike demeanor was a passionate and daring woman. One to equal her aunt.

"Aunt Myrt has a reputation. People in Marshallton understand that she's . . . well, she's eccentric." Leah sat in the soft green leather chair behind her desk.

"Taylor seems to like her." Judd leaned back in the chair, waiting to see Leah's reaction.

"The feeling seems mutual," Leah admitted. "But then Aunt Myrt has always liked men."

"And you don't?"

"Mr. Barnett—"

"Your aunt told me this morning that you've been too busy keeping her out of the asylum and raising and educating your younger half brother and sister to have time for a man in your life." Judd remembered every word Myrtle Mae Derryberry had told him about her niece. He knew the old woman was trying to play matchmaker, and he found the

THE WANDERER 33

thought amusing. What a pair he and Leah would make. The lady and the tramp.

"Where did you see my aunt?" Dear Lord, what had Aunt Myrt said? How much personal information had she given this man—this perfect stranger?

"At your house this morning for breakfast."

"My house . . . for breakfast?"

"I stopped by there with Taylor, and Myrtle Mae insisted we both join her for breakfast. It was just coffee and corn-flakes and some of your homemade blueberry muffins. You're a good cook."

This can't be happening, she thought. Was her aunt so determined to keep her away from Stanley that she was willing to throw her into the arms of the nearest man? And not just any man, but a homeless wanderer—a man with a thick beard, overly long hair, faded jeans, patched shirt and tattered jacket. "Is Taylor still with Aunt Myrt?"

"I'm not sure if they're still together or not. She was going to take him around and introduce him to some of her friends. She was pretty sure she could find him a couple of odd jobs." Judd leaned over, dropping his big hands between his spread knees. "Speaking of jobs . . ."

"What do you know about Mr. Taylor?" Leah asked. Although the older man had appeared to be a gentleman last night, there was always the possibility that he might take advantage of Aunt Myrt's kindness.

"I've only known him a couple of weeks. I met him in Jackson. It was a cool night and we shared what was left of a fifth of rum with some other poor soul." Judd knew something of Taylor's background, enough to respect the man and be fairly certain he would never hurt anyone, least of all a sweet old lady like Myrtle Mae.

"Then you don't really know him? You can't tell me anything about him?"

"Don't worry about your aunt. Taylor's an honest man, and he'll tell her about himself when the time is right." Judd stood up, took several steps and slammed down his hands

34   THE WANDERER

atop Leah's desk. "Look, I didn't come here to discuss your
aunt's romance with Taylor. All I want to know is if the job
offer's still open." He couldn't explain to himself what he
was doing here. He should have left town this morning, but
he'd spent a sleepless night wondering what Leah's dark hair
would look like loosened from its bun and spread over a soft
white pillow.

"If you will recall, I didn't offer you a job." Leah found
herself leaning forward, her face only inches from Judd's.
She tilted up her chin. A tingling sensation ran from her
throat to her stomach. Dammit all, how could this man's
presence raise her temperature to sizzling when Stanley
Woolton left her absolutely cold?

He leaned down closer until only a couple of inches separated them. "Are you saying that you don't want me to
work for you?"

She could feel his warm breath, smell the earthy masculine scent of him, and see the dare in his cinnamon-brown
eyes. "It's only a part-time job from now until January. The
pay is minimum wage. No benefits. It's ideal for a teenager
or a retiree, but I hardly think a man your age would be interested."

He didn't move away from her, but stayed close, his lips
hovering over hers when he replied. "I haven't held down a
steady job in over three years. I've been wandering around
the country, living off odd jobs. I've worked for a few
hours, for weeks or a couple of months, everywhere from
Chattanooga to Dallas. I'm not too proud to take the kind
of job you're offering. But then, you aren't offering it, are
you?"

"I...er...I..."

"What are you so afraid of, Ms. Marshall?"

When he moved closer, his lips almost touching hers, she
jerked backward, her eyes wide, her mouth agape. She
jumped up out of her chair, quickly placing herself behind
it. "I don't know what you're talking about. I...I have a job
opening. You need a job. I pay once a week. On Fridays. In

THE WANDERER 35

cash. You come to work at nine, have an hour for lunch and leave work at six. You can start in the morning if you'd like."

"I'd like to start today," he said, moving away from the desk toward the door. "That would give me a day and a half pay by tomorrow, and I need the money."

"Mr. Barnett?"

He opened the door, then turned to face her. "Yeah?"

"I could advance you—"

"No. I'll do the work first. After all, how do you know you can trust me?" He walked out of the office.

Leah shook her head, uncertain what had just happened. She'd had no intention of hiring the man, and she'd gone and done just that. Had she lost her mind? How was she going to deal with him? For a poor vagrant, he was arrogant, ill-mannered and... and he stirred to life something within her that she preferred to ignore.

When she walked out of her office, she found Judd waiting for her, but all his attention seemed focused on Todd Wilson. Leah glanced at the child, then back at Judd. What was it about Milly's little boy that affected Judd so strongly?

"I'm going to carry Milly's package out to her car for her," Pattie called out. "She has her hands full with this one."

"Fine," Leah said, then turned to Judd. "Don't you like children, Mr. Barnett?"

He didn't look at her when he responded. "I like children, as long as they belong to someone else."

For the life of her she couldn't explain why his answer not only surprised her, but upset her. "I see."

He glanced at her, his face solemn. "If I'm going to be working for you, don't you think you should call me Judd?"

"Yes, certainly...Judd."

"And, of course, you'll want me to call you Ms. Marshall."

Noticing the edges of his mouth turn up slightly and the glint in his dark eyes, she knew he was making fun of her. "Good breeding, genteel manners and proper etiquette are undoubtedly things someone like you finds amusing, but I can assure you that one doesn't necessarily have to have money to possess these things. I come from a fine family, but not a rich one. I'm a woman who works for a living. Works very hard. I've spent a lifetime providing for myself and my family and I—"

He reached out, cupping her chin in the curve between his thumb and forefinger. "Don't get so riled up, ma'am. I admit that I was poking a little fun at you, but I can assure you that I hold you in the highest regard. Especially after everything that Myrtle Mae told me about you." He hadn't been able to resist making that last statement even though he knew it would send her into a tailspin. And he couldn't resist touching her.

His grip on her chin was firm but gentle. His hand was huge. She felt as if it had encompassed her entire face. She looked at him. Her breath caught in her chest, creating a mounting pressure. "What... what did Aunt Myrt tell you about me?"

"Everything." He ran his hand down her throat, stopping at her collar bone before releasing her.

"Everything?" Dear Lord, surely Aunt Myrt hadn't told him about her plans to marry and have a child by the time she turned forty.

"Relax," he said, not touching her, but his gaze stroked her as surely as his hands could have. "All your secrets are safe with me."

He didn't know any of Leah's secrets. Not yet. All Myrtle Mae had told him was the basic facts of Leah's life. How her own mother had died when Leah had been a small child. How her father had remarried a little tramp who'd given him two more children and, when he'd died unexpectedly of a heart attack in his forties, she had run off, leaving a twenty-one-year-old Leah to support and raise her younger

THE WANDERER 37

siblings. Myrtle Mae had admitted that her former brother-in-law and the little tramp had tried to have her committed to an asylum. But Leah, strong and competent and caring, had sacrificed her own personal hopes and dreams for the sake of those she loved—her aunt, her sister and her brother.

Leah's life, Judd decided, had been the exact opposite of his. Where Leah had given all she had to give to her family, Judd had given his all to making himself a multimillionaire, practically ignoring his irresponsible, young wife and his only child. His greed for power and wealth had cost Steven his life.

"Hey, there," Pattie Cornell said as she reentered the shop. "Why don't you introduce me to this gorgeous man?"

Leah groaned. Judd laughed. Pattie glowed.

"Mr. Bar...Judd, this is Pattie Cornell, a dear friend of mine and my full-time employee here at Country Class." Leah didn't like the way Judd and Pattie were smiling at each other. "Pattie." Leah enunciated both syllables, moving her body closer to her friend so that she could jab her gently in the ribs. "This is Judd Barnett. He's going to be our handyman and deliveryman during the holidays."

Pattie threw up her hands and popped them on her jaws in a mock show of surprise. "Will wonders never cease. I thought we'd be stuck with some pimple-face adolescent or Pa Kettle again."

"I'm glad you approve, Ms. Cornell," Judd said.

Leah hated the smooth friendliness in Judd's voice, and hated even more the very intimate way he was looking at Pattie.

"Call me Pattie. After all, we're going to be fellow workers. Besides, we don't stand on ceremony around here, do we, Leah?"

Leah forced a smile. She thought she was going to be sick. She'd seen Pattie *operate* before and had always found it fascinating the way she charmed men. But Leah didn't want her flirting with Judd. My goodness, couldn't she see that he was just a bum? His clothes might be fairly clean, but

38   THE WANDERER

they were nearly rags. And he might be big and tall and good-looking, but he badly needed a haircut and a shave.

"If you want to start today, then I think now is as good a time as any," Leah said, the phony smile still plastered across her face. "I have a pine hall tree that needs to be delivered to Mrs. Humphreys. It should fit in my station wagon."

"You don't use your station wagon for all your deliveries, do you?" Judd asked.

"For everything except the really big pieces of furniture," Pattie said, gazing up at him, her long eyelashes fluttering. "Then we borrow Fred Carter's truck."

"Fred Carter?" Judd thought Pattie Cornell was delightful. And she was harmless. He knew, even if Leah didn't have the vaguest idea, that Pattie was doing her level best to upset Leah by flirting with him.

"Fred owns the Furniture Mart over on Vine Street. He's...sort of...one of my boyfriends." Pattie glanced at Leah. "I've got half a dozen. A smart woman always keeps a few spares. That's what I've been trying to tell Leah for years, but..." Pattie released a long, dramatic sigh. "Leah just has Weasel...er...I mean Stanley. He does have plenty of money, and his mother belongs to all the right clubs, and he is as—"

"Pattie, I don't think Judd is interested in your social life or mine." If she could get Pattie alone for five minutes, she was going to strangle her.

"Right. Sorry." Pattie dropped her head forlornly, but gave Judd a wink. "Aunt Myrt and I have been trying to get Leah to expand her horizons a little."

"My station wagon is parked in the back alley," Leah said, determined to change the subject. "The keys are on my desk and the hall tree is in the back storeroom."

Judd turned to Pattie, completely ignoring Leah. "I'd love to take you to lunch today, but since I'm a little short on funds, how about lunch a week from today?"

THE WANDERER

"I'd love to," Pattie said. "Why don't you let me treat you today?"

"Do you mind, Ms. Marshall?" Judd asked.

"Why should I mind?" Leah said, her breathing quick and labored. "Just deliver Mrs. Humphreys's hall tree and you and Pattie can go...anywhere." Why, Leah wondered, had the words *can go to hell for all I care* jumped to her mind?

"See you in about thirty minutes," Pattie said, and blew Judd a kiss before returning to the front of the shop.

"Give me Mrs. Humphreys's address and directions, and I'll be on my way," Judd said.

"The address is on the sales slip attached to the hall tree. It's the third house on Tipton. A cedar-and-brick house. Tipton is two blocks off Main street." Leah refused to look at him. She didn't want to take the chance that he might detect the anger and frustration she felt. "Just wait here and I'll get my keys."

Leah heard the front door open, but didn't turn around, knowing Pattie could take care of any customers.

"Well, good afternoon, Mrs. Woolton," Pattie said, loudly projecting her voice. "How may I help you?"

Leah jerked around quickly to see Cora Woolton giving Pattie a condescending appraisal. She knew Cora didn't approve of Pattie's miniskirts, skintight blue jeans, abundance of costume jewelry or her use of makeup.

"I need to speak to Leah." Cora's voice held that frosty, superior tone that proclaimed her impatience with *the hired help*.

Just as Leah turned to Judd, hoping she could maneuver him into the storeroom before Stanley's mother saw him, Cora spotted her. Leah smiled and nodded.

"Please go in the storeroom," Leah whispered.

"I don't have the keys to the wagon," Judd said.

"I'll get them for you in a few minutes. Please, go in the storeroom."

"Now?"

40   THE WANDERER

"Yes, now..." But it was too late, Cora was fast approaching. Leah closed her eyes and said a silent prayer.

"Leah, dear, I need a few moments of your time to... oh..." Cora glared at Judd, wrinkling her nose as if she smelled something unpleasant.

"Judd, the keys are on my desk," Leah said, smiling all the while her stomach stirred with nausea. "Get them and then load the wagon."

"Yes, ma'am. I'll get right on it." Judd bowed his head, playing the humble servant to the hilt. "Now, ma'am, don't you worry. I'll be sure to take the delivery to the back door, and I'll wipe my feet before stepping inside the house, and I'll certainly thank Mrs. Humphreys for doing business with us...with you...er...with Country Class, that is."

"Fine, Judd. You can go now."

"Yes, ma'am."

Finally Judd made his exit, but not before Cora Woolton had inspected him from head to toe and, by the look on her face, had found him sadly lacking.

"Who on earth is that man?" Cora asked. "He looks like a hobo."

"He's my...he's the new part-time worker I've hired for the holiday season."

"Oh, my dear. Wherever did you find him?"

"He's a friend of one of Aunt Myrt's friends." Leah wondered just how long it would take the news of Myrtle Mae Derryberry's latest faux pas to spread through Marshallton. After all, Aunt Myrt was bound to tell as many people as possible about her great adventure last night, and how she and Leah had found a couple of Prince Charmings among a group of vagrants.

"I thought you were going to hire Densil Potter's son."

"He's already found a job."

Leah and Cora turned at the sound of the office door opening. They watched Judd as he came out. He bowed, a low, sweeping bow, then went into the storeroom.

THE WANDERER 41

"What was that all about?" Cora asked. "He certainly is a strange man. Of course, if he's a friend of Myrtle Mae's..."

"Cora, you might as well hear it from me since word is bound to reach you sooner or later."

"What is it, dear?"

"Judd is a homeless person. Aunt Myrt and I had a flat tire last night and he was kind enough to fix it for us. Aunt Myrt offered him this job, and...well...I really felt I had no other choice. You understand?"

Cora placed her fat little hand on Leah's arm, patting her gently. "That woman, that woman. Why you haven't had her committed, I don't know. But, Leah, that man..."

"He seems trustworthy. And he does need the job." Leah hated being in this position. She didn't want to have to defend Judd to Stanley's mother.

"You've made a terrible mistake," Cora said. "For all you know this man could well be the person responsible for that robbery over at Ideal Drugs two days ago."

"Surely, you don't think—"

"Stanley said just yesterday that Marshallton is going to have to do something about the growing number of homeless. If I had my way, we'd have Chief Rayburn run them all out of town." Cora squeezed Leah's arm tightly. "Get rid of that man. He'll be nothing but trouble for you. Mark my word."

Leah hated it when Cora Woolton got up on her high horse and started spouting out some asinine nonsense that not only proved she was one of the biggest snobs in town, but one of the most ignorant.

"You said you came by to see me about something?" Leah wanted to divert Cora's attention away from Judd and on to something—anything—else.

"I wanted to let you know that the committee for the charity ball will be meeting at my house tonight at seven-thirty."

"Tonight?"

42 THE WANDERER

"I know it's short notice, but tonight will be convenient for Stanley."

"Fine. I'll be there."

"Are you free for lunch, dear?" Cora asked. "I'm joining Stanley at Merritt's, and I'm sure he'd love to see you."

Leah glanced around Cora, noting a frowning Pattie shaking her head. "I'm afraid Pattie has a lunch date in about thirty minutes, Cora. Please give Stanley my best."

The moment Cora Woolton closed the front door behind her, Pattie let out a loud groan. "That woman is positively nauseating. Even if you think you could spend the rest of your life with Weasel Woolton pawing you, how do you imagine you could live with that narrow-minded old shrew?"

"I admit that Cora is a bit much at times—"

"A bit much? She practically accused Judd Barnett of being a thief just because he's poor and homeless. How could you just stand there and let her say those things?"

"I hardly think it's my place to defend a man I barely know to one of Marshallton's most upstanding citizens."

"Leah, we've known each other for years and I love you like a sister, but sometimes . . ."

"Sometimes what?" Leah knew the minute she asked that she'd made a mistake. Pattie was a lot of things, but subtle wasn't one of them. Asking her a direct question was always dangerous.

"Judd Barnett, despite the fact that you obviously are scared to death to admit it, has your heart all aflutter."

Leah gasped, but before she could verbally protest, Pattie continued. "Don't try to deny it. Milly and I are both red-blooded females and he certainly got the adrenaline pumping in us. He may be a bit rough around the edges, honey, but Judd Barnett is one tempting hunk of male flesh. That man is *all* man."

"Just because you found it necessary to drool all over him doesn't mean I find him the least bit attractive," Leah lied to her friend, but she could no longer lie to herself. Pattie

THE WANDERER 43

was right. Judd Barnett was all man, and Leah wasn't used to dealing with his type.

"You're not telling me the truth."

"Pattie!"

"Come on and just admit that he started your motor the same way he did Milly's and mine."

"There is a possibility that beneath his ragged clothes and awful beard an attractive man exists," Leah admitted. "But his manners are atrocious. And...and he makes me nervous."

"Do you want me to point out all your good qualities to him when we have lunch?" Pattie asked, giggling.

"No, I do not."

The sound of the storeroom door opening alerted Leah and Pattie to Judd's presence.

"I'm leaving now, Ms. Marshall," he said.

"Oh, my God, he's still here." Leah felt the rush of embarrassment spread through her, tinting her cheeks a bright pink.

"He probably heard every word we said."

Pattie started giggling again, but her instantaneous laughter wasn't contagious. Leah failed to see the humor in the situation. A sharp pain shot through her right temple. She rubbed the side of her head. Finally, after all the years of struggling to support and educate Larry and Lisa, Leah was on her own—except for Aunt Myrt—and she was determined to marry and have a child before it was too late. Stanley was a widower with a teenage son. A gentle, easygoing man who was liked and respected. Even the people who remembered him from high school as Weasel Woolton could find little fault in Stanley. And he'd been paying court to Leah for months now. He was good company. Intelligent. Well-read. But not once had Stanley's good-night kiss created butterflies in Leah's stomach.

When Judd Barnett just looked at her, an army of butterflies fought World War III in her stomach.

Three

"This was quite a treat, my boy," Taylor said, finishing off the last bites of his sausage biscuit. "It's not often I get taken out for breakfast."

"Since we've both been working, at least we can eat, even if we can't afford a cheap motel room," Judd said.

"I don't mind so much living outside in warm weather, but it can get awfully uncomfortable on cold nights like we've been having lately."

"Lucky for us that the Congregational church sponsors a local shelter, huh?" Judd made a mental note to instruct his brother to send a generous donation to the shelter that had been providing occasional meals and a nightly bed for Taylor and himself. Over the past few years Judd had made certain that Barnett, Inc. became a benefactor to each and every homeless shelter that had given him sanctuary.

"Well, we can only stay through Christmas." Taylor picked up his coffee cup, downing the remainder of warm liquid. "Brother Brown told me that there just aren't

THE WANDERER 45

enough beds to go around, so they have to set up rules, specify how many weeks a person can stay.''

''Maybe by Christmas we'll have enough saved up to share a room over at the Dixie Motel.'' Judd chuckled, thinking about the shabby motel on the far side of town. Back in Memphis he had a mansion sitting empty. An unused Rolls, a Ferrari and a fifty-seven Chevy were parked in the four-car garage. But he had left all of that behind the day he'd put his brother in charge of Barnett, Inc.—the day he'd started running from his past.

''Well, there isn't much call for yard work this late in the year,'' Taylor said. ''Myrtle Mae has been asking around, trying to find me more work, but there just doesn't seem to be any jobs available.''

''You and I are better off than some. At least neither of us has a family to support.'' Before Steven's death, Judd hadn't been aware of what it was like for a man to lose his job and find himself on the streets with a wife and children. But he knew now. For three years he'd been sharing his life with countless strangers whose lives were filled with loneliness and hunger and despair. He'd found that few were worthless and lazy. Some were mentally or physically ill. Countless were drug abusers. But many were ordinary people who'd been forced by circumstances to join the ranks of the homeless.

''Everyone should have a family. It was the one regret in our lives that Sarah and I never had a child. Children would have been so much comfort to Sarah in her last days.'' Taylor's eyes misted with tears. Clearing his throat, he smiled at Judd. ''You're still young enough to start a family. Young enough for a second chance at life.''

Judd had not discussed his past with Taylor. He didn't talk about his past with any of the friends he made along the way. He wanted nothing more than to forget that he'd ever had a son, but the anger and pain and guilt never left him. ''Looks like you're the one getting a second chance. Myrtle Mae seems crazy about you.''

Taylor laughed, the sound deep and hardy. "Some people would say that Myrtle Mae is just plain crazy, but she's the first woman since my Sarah died that's made me feel whole again."

"She's unique, all right." Judd motioned for the waitress to refill his cup.

"When that little plump bundle of energy smiles at me, I feel twenty again." Taylor held out his cup for a refill when the waitress came over with the coffeepot.

"Hey, aren't you the man who was in here a week or so ago dancing with that red-headed woman? Miss Derryberry?" the waitress asked.

"I plead guilty." Taylor winked at the young girl, who immediately burst into laughter before moving along to the next table.

"Are you planning on sticking around here for long?" Judd wondered what it would be like to stay in any one place longer than a couple of months. He knew that Taylor had been on the streets longer than he had.

"If I could find suitable employment, I might consider making Marshallton my permanent residence. A pretty woman can give a man all kinds of ideas." Taylor leaned back in his chair, crossed his arms over his broad chest and began studying his breakfast companion. "Are you going to tell me that you've been working for Myrtle Mae's niece over a week now and you haven't been affected by her big blue eyes or her sweet smile?"

"Oh, Leah affects me all right," Judd said. "I admit that I'd like to wilt the starch in her collar, but the truth of the matter is, Taylor old pal, Leah Marshall has been waiting a long time for a man and she deserves better than me."

Taylor cupped his chin between his thumb and forefinger, scratching the white stubble on his face as he contemplated. "Myrtle Mae is afraid Leah's going to settle for this Stanley Woolton character. I haven't had the privilege of meeting him yet, but from what I hear, I'd say you were a better man for Leah than he is."

THE WANDERER 47

"Wrong," Judd said. "He can offer her marriage where I can offer her nothing but a few weeks of trouble. Besides, my boss lady doesn't quite approve of me."

"Morning, gentlemen," a loud, country-southern voice said.

Judd and Taylor glanced up to see a slender, well-groomed man in his early forties standing beside their table. From his uniform it wasn't difficult to figure out that he was a policeman.

"Hello, officer," Taylor said. "Fine day, isn't it?"

"You two live around these parts, do you?" the policeman asked.

"Is there some particular reason you're asking?" Judd looked directly at the man who stood with one hand on the back of Judd's chair and the other on his slim hip where his gun holster rested.

"Just curious," the man said. "Haven't seen y'all around before and I know just about everybody in Marshallton."

"We're visiting. Temporarily." Judd shifted in his chair, diverting his attention from the policeman to Taylor. "I'm Judd Barnett and this is Mr. Taylor."

"I'm Lieutenant McMillian. I heard you two were part of our vagrant problem, and I thought you might like to know that Marshallton has enough homeless of her own without drifters coming into town adding to the situation."

"Well, Judd, my boy, it seems someone has reported us to the law," Taylor said. "I wonder who would have done such a thing?"

"We're both working," Judd said as he motioned for the waitress. "And we've found shelter, thanks to the Congregational church, so unless you're accusing us of a crime, I don't think we've got anything else to talk about."

The waitress laid the bill on the table, then smiled at the lieutenant. "Hi, Mac. You ready for your pancakes?"

"Be ready in a minute, sugar. You run along until I finish talking to these men, here." McMillian smiled at the waitress, but a scowl crossed his face when he turned back

48 THE WANDERER

to Judd. "We've had two robberies in the past ten days. You two been in town about ten days."

"I do believe this gentleman is implying that we're involved in criminal activities," Taylor said.

Judd stood, his massive body towering over the short, thin McMillian. "I'd say you've got a case of coincidence." The lieutenant moved aside as Judd stepped around him.

Taylor scratched the back of his head and grunted. "If you catch the thieves, you'll let us know, won't you, Mac?"

"You two a couple of smart alecks?" Mac turned and followed Judd toward the door. "Well, you better listen up, boy. As long as you and your buddy over there hang around these parts, the Marshallton police department is going to be keeping tabs on you."

Judd handed the bill to the manager of Hamburger Heaven who was manning the cash register. He pulled out his worn leather wallet, paid the bill and threw up his hand in a goodbye salute to Taylor.

Once outside in the crisp morning air, Judd inhaled deeply, taking the sharp cold air into his lungs. Dammit, he'd had to deal with idiots like McMillian before in more than one town, but this was the first time a policeman had ever suspected him of theft. Judd knew that if he had any sense he'd leave Marshallton today. There was nothing keeping him here.

He walked across the road to the pay telephone, delved into his jeans pocket for a quarter and dropped the coin into the slot. After dialing, he waited. And while he waited he thought about what he was going to say.

"Barnett, Incorporated. Jared Barnett's office. May I help you?" The voice was polite and precise.

"Helen, this is Judd. Put me through to my brother, please."

"Yes, Mr. Barnett."

It had been nearly two months since Judd had spoken to Jared, and he knew his brother would be worried. When

THE WANDERER

49

he'd first left Memphis three and a half years ago, he hadn't gotten in touch with Jared for almost eight months. His hotheaded little brother had been on the verge of hiring private detectives. So now he tried to phone in at least every other month.

"Mr. Barnett, your brother will be with you momentarily," Helen said. "He's just finishing negotiations with Ms. Cochran."

"What would he have to negotiate with Carolyn?" Judd asked, puzzled that his brother would be having a business meeting with his ex-wife. Carolyn didn't have an ounce of business sense.

"Not Carolyn Cochran..." Helen hesitated, as if uncertain how Judd would react to the mention of his former wife. "Bess Cochran, Carolyn's sister."

"Bessie? Little Bessie? What—"

"Judd!" Jared's voice was deep and husky, but it had a scratchy quality that made him sound hoarse all the time. "Dammit, man, it's about time you called in."

"Something wrong?"

"Hell yes, something's wrong. David Cochran died a month ago. You can well imagine what his death did to Carolyn. You know how close she was to her father."

"God, I'm sorry." Judd clutched the phone tightly in one hand while pounding the side of the mini-booth with his other fist. "What happened?"

"Heart attack."

"David was a good man. He taught me a lot about the hotel business." Judd remembered the strong, robust man he'd first met when he and Carolyn's father had become business partners over ten years ago. "I guess that's why Bess has come back to Memphis."

"We haven't seen her in ten years and now she's come home and taken over."

"When you see Carolyn—" For the first time since Steven's death, Judd actually wanted to see his ex-wife. Carolyn was weak and self-centered and totally irresponsible. She

50   THE WANDERER

was like a child who needed constant attention and supervision. He'd cared for her once. Even now he didn't hate her. A part of him wished that he could comfort her. "Tell her how sorry I am about David."

"Yeah, I'll do that," Jared said. "I don't suppose you'd like to come home yourself and help us out. Bess Cochran is trying to make waves."

"You can handle little Bessie. You always could."

"Come home for Christmas."

"I'm in Marshallton. It's a small town not far from Jackson. I've got a job as a handyman and deliveryman until January."

"How long are you going to keep running?" Jared asked.

"As long as it takes."

"Don't spend more than's in your checking account. Remember what happened the last time." Leah gave her aunt a hug, then kissed her on the cheek.

"Well, I think everyone was quite nice about the matter." Myrt stood in front of the carved pine oval mirror, fluffing the ends of her shoulder-length hair. Suddenly she stopped primping, whirled around and shook her index finger at Leah. "Except that nasty little reporter for the *Marshallton Weekly*. He implied that I was writing bad checks, and I did no such thing. In my mother's day, a man could have been horsewhipped for degrading a lady's reputation that way."

Leah patted Myrt on the back, remembering those horrible days when Myrtle Mae's extravagance had put them deeper in debt. After Leah had made good on all of the checks and paid all the fees, she'd had the unpleasant task of dealing with Harry Templeton—that mealymouthed little wart of a reporter. Once Leah had spoken to Howard Davenport, the *Marshallton Weekly*'s owner and an old fraternity brother of her father's, Harry had been forced to print a retraction. But it really hadn't mattered to anyone

THE WANDERER 51

except Myrtle Mae and Leah. The sordid little incident had only further added to Myrt's reputation as a lunatic.

"Don't worry, Leah," Pattie said as she slipped her arms into the sleeves of her red fake-fur jacket. "I'll keep a close watch on Aunt Myrt. We're going to have a fun day shopping in Memphis. I'm going to take her to Paulette's for lunch."

Leah gave Myrt another hug, then turned to Pattie, bending her head close enough so she could whisper to her friend. "Whatever you do, don't let her out of your sight."

"We'll be like Siamese twins. I promise."

Leah picked up a pair of black leather gloves from the top of the checkout counter and handed them to her aunt. "Don't forget these." Leah took Myrt's plump yet fragile little hands into hers. "Do not spend any of your money on me. Is that understood?"

"But you've been wanting some of your favorite perfume for such a long time."

"You can't afford it." When Myrt tilted her head and smiled, Leah shook her finger in Myrt's face. "No, no, no."

"Then what can I afford to get you for Christmas?"

All three women turned immediately when the front door of Country Class swung open. Judd Barnett came barreling in, rubbing up and down on his arms in an effort to warm himself. "Morning, ladies," he said, then cupped his bare hands, covered his mouth and blew his warm breath into his palms.

"Morning, Judd," Pattie said, looking back and forth from Judd to Leah.

Leah had the insane notion to go over, take Judd's hands in hers and warm them against her body. It bothered her to see him with no hat, gloves or scarf. She'd thought about buying him all three items, but had known he wouldn't accept them. In less than ten days, she'd found out that Judd Barnett was a proud man. He'd refused an advance on his paycheck. He had insisted on Leah deducting from his pay the cost of a glass figurine he'd accidently broken, even

52   THE WANDERER

though she had assured him that there was no need. And yesterday morning when he'd brought in cream-filled doughnuts to go with their morning coffee and Leah had offered to reimburse him, he'd acted highly insulted.

"Judd, I don't want you to forget that you're joining us for Christmas," Aunt Myrt said, slipping her hands into her gloves. "I am so looking forward to the holidays this year. Just think, it will be mine and Taylor's first Christmas together."

"Yes, ma'am." Judd stopped outside the storeroom. He glanced at Leah and caught her staring at him. He couldn't count the times in the past week that he'd found her watching him, studying him, as if he were some rare specimen that she longed to put under a microscope.

He'd like to put her under something, but it wasn't a microscope. Leah, with her quiet, courteous manners and her cool superiority had Judd's stomach tied in knots. Although she was highly intelligent and somewhat refined, she lacked the sophistication he'd sought in women before his marriage to Carolyn. And Leah certainly was nothing like the women he'd met since he'd started wandering.

"Don't worry about us if we aren't home until eight or nine tonight," Pattie said as she took Myrt by the arm, escorting her to the front door.

"Please drive carefully." Leah knew Aunt Myrt would be safe with Pattie, but what worried Leah was wondering how safe Pattie would be with Aunt Myrt. "And call if you have any problems."

"You worry too much," Myrt said, waving first to Leah, then to Judd.

"There aren't going to be any problems, are there, Aunt Myrt?" Pattie opened the front door, gave Leah a wide-eyed, reassuring look and hurried Myrt outside to her warm, waiting car.

Once the door closed, Leah took a deep breath. Judd walked into the storeroom, hung his jacket on the hook alongside Leah's coat, then went over to the coffeemaker

THE WANDERER 53

and poured the hot liquid into two mugs. He found Leah
fussing over an arrangement of grapevine wreaths hanging
on the left wall. When he neared her, she turned around,
giving him that shy, sweet smile that made him want to kiss
her. Leah was such a pleasant woman. Always smiling. Often humming or whistling while she worked. And so friendly
to everyone—except him.

Judd handed her one of the coffee mugs. Their hands
touched briefly when the mug went from his grasp to hers.
Leah's gaze flew up, meeting his. She pulled away so quickly
that the coffee sloshed over the sides of the mug. Instantly
she took the mug by the handle, barely avoiding being
burned by the steaming brew.

"Where are Pattie and Myrtle Mae headed?" Judd asked.

"To Memphis to do a little Christmas shopping." Leah
held the mug to her lips, taking a quick sip of the coffee.

"You're afraid Myrtle Mae's going to get Pattie in trouble, aren't you?" Judd's deep baritone laughter sounded
like a groaning chuckle.

"They'll be fine. Pattie's taken Aunt Myrt shopping before." Leah turned to go toward the front of the shop, but
stopped when she heard Judd following her. She turned and
faced him.

Judd's big hands surrounded the coffee mug. He stared
at her. "Look, I appreciate Myrtle Mae's invitation to
Christmas dinner, but I know you'd rather I didn't show up,
so—"

"Don't be silly." Leah avoided any eye contact with him.
"Taylor will be there, so I see no reason for you not to
come, too."

"Are you sure?"

"I'm sure," she said. "Now that that's settled, let's get to
work. I'm expecting a new order of cross-stitched Christmas stockings and that pine-scented spray we ran out of last
week. And you'll have to borrow Fred's truck to deliver the
Myers's bedroom suite. As soon as we get it out of the
storeroom, we can move all those boxes back upstairs."

54   THE WANDERER

"Yes, ma'am."

"Oh, and Judd. I brought my lunch today since I won't
be able to leave the shop. I have more than enough for two,
if you'd care to join me." She'd made the same offer last
week on Pattie's off day and he'd turned her down, saying
that he'd made plans to eat with Taylor.

He watched her closely, trying to gage the sincerity of her
invitation. He'd learned that Leah had a warm and com-
passionate heart. Despite the fact that she seemed to thor-
oughly disapprove of him, he knew that she worried about
him. "Thanks, Ms. Marshall. I'd like to share your lunch."

Leah didn't allow herself to smile until Judd went into the
storeroom. For the life of her, she couldn't explain why she
found herself wanting to reach out to Judd, wanting to truly
get to know him, longing to take him in her arms and ease
the pain she saw in his eyes.

Judd poured the coffee while Leah laid thick slices of
homemade chocolate-chip pound cake on pink-flowered
earthenware plates and placed a stainless-steel fork beside
each setting. Leaning back slightly in her green leather chair,
Leah picked up her plate and cut into the cake with the edge
of her fork.

Judd set the coffeepot atop the ceramic hot plate on the
side of Leah's desk. He sat back, pulling the wing-back
chair closer to the desk.

Taking a huge bite of cake into his mouth, he moaned,
then swallowed. "I have never tasted anything so good." He
picked up his coffee cup, a pink-flowered mate to the plates.
"Of course those chicken-salad sandwiches were mighty
good, too."

"After you ate the third one, I figured out that you liked
them." Leah had intentionally prepared four sandwiches,
certain a man of Judd's size had an appetite to match. She'd
never forget the way he'd eaten at Hamburger Heaven the
night they met.

THE WANDERER 55

Leah tried not to stare at Judd while he finished his slice of cake and fourth cup of coffee. She knew how often he'd caught her staring at him lately, but she couldn't seem to stop herself. Despite the fact that she knew nothing about him except that he had been jobless and homeless when they met, Leah couldn't deny the fact that she found Judd Barnett fascinating. She had decided that he was not only handsome, but intelligent, hardworking and totally male.

"So your sister is a graphic designer living in Nashville and your brother works for a law firm in Chattanooga." Judd wondered if she had exhausted her mothering instincts on her younger siblings. Would a woman as nurturing as Leah be satisfied to spend the rest of her life without a child of her own? Of course, it didn't matter to him, one way or the other. Leah's life was her own business. Not his. He had enough problems without getting involved in anyone else's.

"That's right. Lisa is unbelievably creative and talented. And Larry was always a straight-A student as well as a fine athlete."

"You sound like a proud mama." Judd set his cup on his empty plate, wiped his hands off on the pink cloth napkin and stood up.

"I guess, in a way, I am like a mother to Larry and Lisa. They were only ten and eight when our father died and Gloria . . . their mother . . . deserted them."

When Leah picked up her plate and cup, Judd reached out, took them and stacked them on top of his. "Here, I'll take those. Let me clean up."

"Thanks." Leah checked her watch. "We've been back here over an hour. It's really been slow today. Not one customer has come in since eleven this morning."

"Things will pick up the closer it gets to Christmas Day." Judd carried the dishes out of the office and into the back storeroom, placing them in a small corner sink.

Leah followed him, checking the row of small boxes waiting to be unpacked. "As soon as you finish, bring these two boxes up front. They're crystal angels and I want to do a display up on that high rack in the front of the shop."

"It won't take me a minute in here."

With one hand, Leah lifted an aluminum stepladder from its storage place in the corner of the room and left Judd to wash the dishes. "There's extra cake in the sack over there. I thought you and Taylor might like some later."

Looking up from where his hands rested in a pile of dish detergent suds, Judd smiled at Leah. "Thanks."

She was so different from any woman he'd ever known. She was strong, caring and responsible. She had brains and breeding, and yet seemed able to manage without the wealth Myrtle Mae had told him their family once possessed, long before Leah's birth.

Judd stacked the plates and cups on the drain rack, dried his hands and folded the pink napkins. Picking up two small boxes, he carried them out into the shop where Leah was already high atop the stepladder.

"That was quick," she said, running a dust rag across the empty top shelf of a ceiling-high display case. "I want to put the angels up here, away from busy little hands. They're very fragile and quite expensive."

Judd ripped open a box with his pocket knife. When he uncrated the first delicate crystal angel, he held it up in his hand, allowing the fluorescent light from the overhead fixture to sparkle off the exquisitely sculpted ornament. "Very pretty," he said, handing an angel to Leah.

She enclosed the small figurine in her hand and placed it on the shelf. "I've been collecting angels since I was a little girl. For the past few years, I've had enough to decorate a whole Christmas tree."

Judd handed Leah another angel. "An angel tree, huh?"

One by one Leah placed the angels on the top shelf. Judd opened the second box. She readjusted her position on the ladder, then reached out for the next ornament. He held out another angel. She reached to take it, but the exchange fell short and the delicate glass angel slipped through her fin-

THE WANDERER

gers. She reached down, trying to grab it before it hit the floor, and she inadvertently lost her balance. Judd shot out his big hand, hoping to catch the falling angel, but it bounced off his open palm and crashed to the floor.

"Sorry," he said, turning his attention to Leah. Suddenly he realized that she was falling from her perch on the top rung of the ladder.

"Judd!" Leah cried out just as she dropped into his open arms.

Despite the fact that Leah wasn't a tiny woman, she was a lightweight to hold. She was warm and soft and fit perfectly into his arms. He couldn't resist the urge to pull her close. She was breathing heavily, her breasts rising and falling rapidly. She clung to him, her arm about his neck as she grasped his shoulder, her other hand resting against his chest.

Leah knew her heart was racing. She had never been in a man's arms like this, and she found Judd's nearness overwhelmingly erotic. He was so big and strong, and he was holding her as if he never wanted to let her go. She gazed into his eyes, those bronze eyes as dark and cinnamon-brown as his hair and beard, and recognized the look of longing that surely he could see in her own eyes.

This isn't happening, she thought. It couldn't be. She was dating Stanley Woolton with plans to marry the man. How could she allow herself to fall in love with Judd Barnett, a man she barely knew? She wasn't some teenager, some silly schoolgirl. She was almost thirty-nine, and she knew exactly what she did and didn't want in a man. She wanted a reliable, responsible man with a good job and a secure future. Not some drifter, some wanderer who couldn't settle down in one place.

"Leah?" He wasn't sure what he was asking her. For permission to continue holding her? For permission to want her so desperately that he'd like nothing better than to take her back to the storeroom and make love to her? Or maybe for permission to kiss her because he knew, barring an act of God, that was just what he intended to do?

"I'm all right," she said in a tiny whisper. "You can put me down now." But she didn't remove her arm from around his neck or release his shoulder from her grip. Instead she raised her hand from his chest and touched his face.

He drew in his breath on a labored groan. Hell, why had she touched him? The feeling of her small hand resting against his cheekbone and beard ignited a fistful of fireworks inside him. He was getting hard and there wasn't a damn thing he could do about it.

She kept staring at him all the while he was lowering his head, slowly, ever so slowly. When his lips hovered over hers, she draped the back of his head with her hand, running her fingers through the shaggy ends of his long, auburn hair.

"I need this," he whispered against her mouth seconds before he took it, hard and hot and all-consuming. He kissed her as if his very life depended on it.

Leah moaned, opening her mouth for his invasion. She clung to him, helpless yet unafraid of the power, the sheer masculine strength of his possession.

He shifted her weight in his arms, allowing the side of her hip to rest against his arousal, groaning with a hot, wild desire he hadn't known in years. And never this quickly, this completely.

Leah's mind kept trying to warn her about something, but her body refused to allow the message to get through until she felt the undeniable evidence of Judd's passion. She tried to pull her mouth away from his, but he kept kissing her. Finally she tugged on his hair. He opened his eyes, staring at her with a dazed look.

He rested his forehead against hers, then slowly lowered her to her feet, her body still intimately fitted to his. "I'm sorry, Ms. Marshall—"

Leah covered his lips with the tips of her fingers. "Don't you dare ever call me that again. My name is Leah."

THE WANDERER 59

"Leah." Taking her by the shoulders, Judd pushed her a few inches away from him, separating their bodies.

"We need to talk about this," she said, wondering if what had just happened meant as much to him as it had to her.

"I don't want to complicate your life. I don't want to hurt you. Ever. You do believe that, don't you?"

When Judd heard the front door opening, he dropped his hands from her shoulders and glanced over the top of her head. A slender dark-haired man wearing a business suit, a pair of wire-framed glasses and carrying a briefcase walked into the shop.

"What's wrong, Leah?" Stanley Woolton asked, rushing forward, his small black eyes darting back and forth from Leah to Judd to Leah.

"Oh, my God!" Leah groaned quietly.

"It's all right," Judd whispered. "He just now walked in. He didn't see a thing."

Leah turned to face Stanley. "Just a little accident with one of the Christmas ornaments. Judd was fixing to get a broom and clean it up, weren't you, Judd?"

"Yes, ma'am. I'll get the broom and dustpan."

The last thing Judd wanted to do was leave Leah alone with Weasel Woolton, but he had sense enough to know that now wasn't the time to make a stand. He might not have a lifetime commitment to offer Leah, but Myrtle Mae was right. Leah deserved better than a skinny little accountant with a balding head and a high-pitched voice.

"What brings you by here this time of day?" Leah asked, walking hurriedly toward Stanley.

Leaning over, he kissed her on the cheek. His lips were cold and his kiss nothing but a hard peck. "I don't like the idea of your hiring some stranger that you and Myrt picked up off the street, and now that I've seen the man, I'm more certain than ever that you should get rid of him."

"Stanley, I think you're being unreasonable. Judd is a good employee." And a damned good kisser, Leah thought,

60 THE WANDERER

then scolded herself for letting her emotions get the better of her.

"Well, Mac thinks it's a strange coincidence that there've been two robberies since your employee and his friend Mr. Taylor arrived in town." Stanley set his briefcase down atop the checkout counter, adjusted his glasses with the tips of his thumb and forefinger and ran a long, slender hand across the top of his head, straightening the thin strands of his black, windblown hair. "Heed my warning, Leah. Get rid of that man. He's going to prove dangerous."

"Dangerous?" Yes, she thought, Judd Barnett was dangerous. He had already disrupted her well-laid plans, had made her question her own sanity, and was on the verge of capturing her heart.

"Mac says the thieves are amateurs. Marshallton has never had two store break-ins so close together. You'll do well to get rid of that man before he steals you blind."

"I'll do no such thing."

"It isn't like you to be so stubborn," Stanley said, looking at Leah as if he'd just noticed something different about her. "You have an odd look on your face, Leah. Are you ill?"

"Could have been the chicken salad we had for lunch," Judd said, coming out of the storeroom, broom and dustpan in hand.

"You had lunch with him?" Stanley glared at Judd. He puffed out his chest and stood up as tall and straight as a man of his small stature could.

"I brought sandwiches and cake from home," Leah said, then wondered why she was bothering to explain to Stanley. They weren't married. They weren't even engaged.

Stanley motioned for Leah to come close. She glanced around and saw that Judd was ignoring the two of them as he busily cleaned up the shards of broken angel from the floor.

THE WANDERER

"Stanley, you haven't said why you stopped by." Thank goodness he hadn't walked in a few minutes sooner or he would have caught her in Judd's arms.

"Mother wanted me to remind you that you're invited to dinner tonight. She thought we might want to spend some time together before you two have your weekly meeting with the charity-ball committee."

Stanley kept staring at Judd. Leah wondered if Stanley thought the other man was going to steal something while he was watching him. The very idea that Judd was a thief was ludicrous. He had too much pride to steal. "I hadn't forgotten. Tell your mother that I'll be there. Six-thirty sharp. I'll leave straight from here."

"Well, you might want to go home and freshen up," Stanley said, surveying her from head to toe. "For some reason, you look rather mussed."

Leah bit down on her lip and uttered a prayer for patience. "I'll go home and change. We've had a busy morning and I've been—"

"Leah fell off the stepladder," Judd said, propping himself against the broom and holding the dustpan in his hand. "Luckily I was here to catch her, but I'm afraid she did get a little *mussed*."

Stanley's face turned a vivid pink. "You must be more careful, dear." He gave Leah a comforting hug about her shoulders, then whispered, "It must have been dreadful having that man touch you."

"Dreadful? Oh, yes, dreadful," Leah lied.

"Take care now," Stanley said, picking up his briefcase. "I'm having a late lunch with a client. I've got to run. See you tonight."

The minute Stanley left, Judd dropped the broom and walked toward Leah, a maniacal smile on his face.

"Judd...whatever you're thinking about doing... don't."

Leah backed away from him. He kept coming toward her. "You are not going to marry Stanley Woolton."

62   THE WANDERER

"I'm not?"

Judd backed her up against a display case, her hips pressing into the edge. Placing his hands atop the case, one on each side of Leah, he leaned over, pushing his body into hers. "I've decided to stay in Marshallton long enough to make sure you don't ruin your life."

"You have?"

"Yes, I have. You shouldn't settle for the likes of that," Judd said, nodding toward the door that Stanley had only moments ago exited. "There are a lot of men out there who'd consider themselves lucky to have a woman like you."

"Who?" she asked.

"Who what?"

"Who would consider himself lucky to have a woman like me?"

"Any smart man."

"Would you?"

"Would I what?" he asked.

"Would you consider yourself lucky to have a woman like me?"

He studied her face—her big blue eyes, her soft warm lips, her small nose, her flawless complexion. "Yes, ma'am, I'd consider myself the luckiest man alive." And then he leaned just a little closer and kissed her. A tender, seductive kiss, meant to whet her appetite for more.

Four

"**I** thought you said there was nothing going on between you and Judd Barnett." Lisa Marshall smiled at her older sister as she continued stacking dirty plates into the dishwasher.

"Don't let her give you the old song and dance about the two of them just being friends." Pattie Cornell entered the kitchen with a tray of cups and saucers. "You've been around them for a few hours today and you picked up on the chemistry between them. Imagine what it's like for me." Pattie set the tray down on the kitchen table. "I work with them every day. I have to watch Leah pretending that she isn't falling in love."

"I am not falling in love." Leah slammed the large oven roaster against the side of the sink, sloshing sudsy dishwater onto the floor. "Will you two please keep your voices down? Someone could hear you."

"The men are all in the living room," Pattie said, eyeing the spill on the floor. "Want me to get a mop?"

64 THE WANDERER

Leah wiped the suds off her hands, then dried her hands on the oversize apron she wore. "No, I will." She glared at Pattie, then glanced over at her sister. "I don't want you to discuss this in front of Aunt Myrt. She's been trying to play matchmaker since the night she and I met Judd and Taylor."

"Looks like Aunt Myrt has it bad," Lisa said, closing her eyes and sighing. "Ah, love. Wonder what it's like to fall in love at sixty?"

Leah opened the broom closet, grabbed a small sponge mop, then closed the door with her hip. "It's all right for Aunt Myrt to act irresponsibly. It's second nature to her. But I've made up my mind that I want a child before I'm too old to have one. And that requires a good husband and father. A reliable man, a man who can offer a child security."

"Is she talking about Weasel Woolton again?" Lisa asked Pattie. "I thought surely she would have given up on him by now."

"Oh, I think a proposal is definitely in the air." Pattie shrugged as she breathed out on an exaggerated whine. "He's been very attentive for the past few weeks, and Leah has been seeing him as much as possible to avoid facing her real feelings for Judd."

After cleaning up the spilled dishwater, Leah handed the mop to Pattie. "Here, take care of this. Do something constructive instead of filling my sister's head with all sorts of nonsense."

Pattie held the mop as a prop, leaning against it as she turned to Lisa. "Talk to her, will you? I've been trying to tell her that a man like Judd doesn't come along every day. It's so obvious the guy's got the hots for her, but she keeps giving him the cold shoulder."

"I think Pattie's right." Lisa put her hand on Leah's back. "No matter how much you deny it, there is something between you and Judd. I've seen the way he looks at you... the way you look at him. I may not be the most ex-

THE WANDERER

perienced woman in the world, but I know sexual desire when I see it."

"I want more than sexual desire," Leah said, her voice a whispered hiss. "Judd can't offer me what I want."

"Are you sure you know what you want?" Lisa asked.

"I've known the man less than a month." Leah turned back to the pots and pans in the sink, scrubbing on them furiously. "I like Judd...and, yes, I'm attracted to him. But I don't know anything about him, except that...well, that he seems to want me."

"Finally, she admits it!" Pattie shoved the mop back and forth in the air like a majorette's baton.

"What has Leah admitted?" Myrtle Mae asked as she came bouncing into the room.

Leah moaned. Focusing all her attention on the sink of dirty utensils, she ignored her aunt. Lisa's mouth curved into a smile. Pattie giggled.

"My goodness, with that sort of reaction, y'all must have been discussing men." Myrt rummaged around in an above-counter cabinet. "Where are those extra boxes of chocolate-covered cherries? I thought I'd pass them around. Taylor and I just love them, and we're both dying for some."

"They're in the pantry," Leah said, but didn't turn around. "Pattie, get a box out of the pantry for Aunt Myrt. They're on the second shelf on the right."

"Well, have you two persuaded Leah to go with her heart and have an affair with Judd?" Myrt looked from Lisa to Pattie, who had just gone into the pantry.

Leah grasped the handle of the stainless-steel double broiler she held. "Myrtle Mae Derryberry! Of all the things to say."

"Oh, pooh. It isn't against the law to discuss sex," Myrt said. "We're all over twenty-one. We're consenting adults, aren't we?"

"Right you are," Pattie said as she emerged from the pantry and handed Myrt two boxes of chocolate-covered cherries. "And, yes, I think if we took a vote right now,

66 THE WANDERER

everyone in this house would agree that Leah and Judd should...well, should—"

"Have an affair," Lisa said.

"See what I mean?" Jerking her hands out of the dishwater, Leah whirled around to face the others. "You're a bad influence, Aunt Myrt, encouraging my baby sister to make suggestions about my love life."

"Lord knows someone needs to make a few suggestions." Myrt glanced around the room, obviously seeking approval. "Christmas dinner is over. Pattie is taking Lisa and Larry to a party in Jackson, so they'll be leaving shortly. Taylor and I would like to be alone for a while. I *suggest* you take Judd for a ride. Give him a tour of Marshallton. Share the joy of the holiday season. Live dangerously for once."

"I...I had planned to stop by at the Woolton's this evening. Cora invited me to supper." Leah had to admit that she didn't relish the idea of spending several hours with Stanley, who would talk endlessly about his accounting firm and all their many prestigious clients. Nor did she look forward to listening to Cora gossiping about everything and everyone in Marshallton. Least of all was her desire to be around Trey. Aunt Myrt was absolutely right about the boy. He was a spoiled, egotistical little smart aleck.

But being alone with Judd would be unwise. The man made her feel reckless; his very presence was a threat to her self-control.

"Well, if you go over to Cora's, you'll just have to take Judd with you," Myrt said. "Taylor and I want to be alone. We've made plans."

"If I didn't know better," Lisa said, "I'd think you and Mr. Taylor were going to do something naughty."

"Lisa Diane Marshall!" Leah's outburst was mingled with a touch of humor that she couldn't disguise.

"Well, of course we are." Myrt tucked the two boxes of chocolate-covered cherries under her arm and, humming merrily, waltzed out of the room.

"She's priceless," Lisa said.

THE WANDERER 67

"You might as well go ahead and cancel your supper date with the Wooltons." Pattie grinned, deepening the dimples in her round cheeks.

"What am I going to do with her?" Leah laughed, admitting defeat. She had never been able to triumph over Aunt Myrt when the old woman set her mind on a definite objective.

"Don't worry so much about what you're going to do with Myrtle Mae, but about what you're going to do with Judd," Pattie said.

Leah made no reply. She knew her friend was right. Aunt Myrt was a problem she had learned to deal with over the years, but Judd Barnett was another problem altogether. In the past two weeks since she'd fallen off the ladder and they'd exchanged a rather heated kiss, Judd hadn't tried to hide the fact that he wanted to make love to her. And Leah realized that the longer he stayed in her life, the harder it was going to be for her to resist the temptation to give herself to a man she barely knew.

"Well, congratulations, Mr. Taylor," Larry Marshall said. "I think that's wonderful."

"It's been quite a spell since I had a full-time job." Taylor stuck his pipe in the corner of his mouth and lighted the tobacco with the silver lighter Myrt had given him for Christmas. "I still can't believe it." He turned to Judd, who was sitting beside him on the overstuffed floral-print country sofa in Leah's spacious living room. "Judd here heard about the opening over at the Southland Inn. Now, I'm the new desk clerk. I start work tomorrow."

"And they're actually going to provide you with a room?" Larry leaned back in the beige corduroy rocker-recliner, propping his feet on the footrest.

"Unbelievable, huh? And the salary isn't bad. I'll be able to do things for Myrtle Mae now instead of her doing for me." Taylor's weary blue eyes misted.

68 THE WANDERER

"Did I hear someone mention my name?" Myrt asked as she entered the room and held out a box of candy to Taylor.

"You certainly did, my love," Taylor said. "I was just saying that now that I'm gainfully employed, I can wine and dine you in style."

Myrt laughed her sexy throaty laugh that gained her the full attention of all three men in the room. "What about you, Judd? Are you giving any thought to finding full-time work and staying on here in our fair city now that you've discovered what a gem our Leah is?"

"Don't be subtle, Aunt Myrt," Larry said, grinning. "Why don't you just come right out and ask the man what his intentions are concerning Leah?"

"Well, it's really your place to protect Leah since you're the man in the family, but obviously you're a part of this modern generation who doesn't give a hoot about old family values." Myrt set the second box of chocolates down on the coffee table, then squeezed her ample bottom down between Taylor and Judd, snuggling close to the man who was busy unwrapping the other box of candy.

"I don't believe in interfering in other people's lives." Larry twined his fingers together and placed his hands behind his neck as he rested his head on the back of the rocker.

Myrt turned to Judd. "Just what are your intentions concerning Leah?"

Larry bellowed with laughter. Judd smiled, but his cheeks flushed ever so slightly. Taylor offered Myrt a chocolate-covered cherry. Accepting one, she popped it into her mouth, but didn't take her eyes off Judd for a second.

"I like Leah," Judd said. "I don't want to see a woman as wonderful . . . well, as fine as Leah, waste her life married to a man like Stanley Woolton." Judd had a difficult time admitting to himself, let alone anyone else, how deeply his feelings for Leah ran. Not only did he desire her physically, but she stimulated him intellectually and stirred his buried emotions. She was bringing back to life a part of the

THE WANDERER   69

man he'd once been—a hardworking, dependable man, one who didn't shirk his responsibilities.

"Then what do you intend to do about it?" Myrt asked.

Judd glanced at Taylor, who smiled and shrugged, as if to say *you're on your own*. Then Judd turned to Larry, hoping Leah's brother would intervene.

"I'd like to hear your answer myself," Larry said.

"Leah wants marriage," Judd said. "I can't offer her that."

"Maybe. Maybe not." Myrt reached for a second piece of candy. "What Leah wants is well and good, but what Leah needs is of more importance."

"Dare we ask what it is that you think Leah needs?" Larry sat up straight in the rocker, placed his hands atop his thighs and stared directly at Myrt. Strands of his black wavy hair fell down over one eye.

"Leah needs a wild and passionate affair with a man who can teach her what it's like to really be a woman. She needs to experience a grand passion." Myrt popped the chocolate into her mouth.

All three men stared at her, their mouths agape, their eyes wide. Then suddenly Larry started laughing.

"Excellent idea," Taylor said, placing his arm around Myrt's shoulder.

Judd felt a slowly warming heat spread through his entire body. Myrtle Mae had put into words the desire that had been building inside him for weeks. It had been years since he'd wanted a woman so badly—and wanted her to the exclusion of all others. In the long run, he wouldn't be good for Leah Marshall. But, on a temporary basis, he could be better for her than any other man on the face of the earth.

The Christmas lights adorning the downtown decorations shone brightly, but appeared to be nothing more than reflected glimmers in the brilliant December sunlight. This year the holiday season in western Tennessee certainly wasn't enriched with a blanket of snow. Not one flake had been seen this year; not even a drop of rain had fallen in weeks. Except for the bare tree limbs and winter-dark grass, the day possessed the splendor of autumn. A light, unseasonably warm breeze and a blue sky streaked with late-afternoon hues of mauve and lavender and scarlet helped create the illusion.

Leah hadn't spoken a word to Judd since they'd left her house ten minutes earlier. She couldn't figure out exactly how Aunt Myrt had maneuvered matters to suit herself, but she had. Pattie had insisted that she and Larry and Lisa run by and see some old high school friends, who now lived in Finger, before they drove on over to Jackson for tonight's party. The threesome hadn't been gone more than twenty minutes when Aunt Myrt had handed Leah her coat, purse and car keys while Taylor tossed Judd his worn leather jacket. Once outside, Judd had laughed and said, "I'm not sure whose romance they're working on, theirs or ours." Leah hadn't responded. She'd simply given him a hard look.

"Where are we going?" Judd asked as Leah drove out of town, turning onto a two-lane road.

"Does it matter?" Her voice had a snapping, curt edge, but she didn't care. This little drive hadn't been her idea. She did not want to spend time alone with Judd. It wouldn't be safe for either of them. She would either take out on him her anger at Aunt Myrt or she would succumb to his undeniable charm and make a fool of herself.

"Look, if you don't want to be with me, then turn around and go back to town. You can drop me off on any street corner."

Leah clutched the steering wheel, her eyes focused on the narrow road ahead. His words about dropping him off on any street corner reminded her that Judd had no home, no place to go, no one to be with on Christmas Day. "I'm sorry. I...I've been acting childishly. It's just that I had plans...Aunt Myrt simply disregarded my feelings. She's so certain you're going to save me from marrying Stanley."

THE WANDERER

Turning toward her, Judd placed his arm across the seat, his fingers almost touching Leah's tense shoulder. "Did you hear what you just said?" he asked, not a trace of humor in his voice.

"What?" She stole a quick glance at him, and her heart stopped for one brief instant. He was so big and tall and totally male that he seemed too large for the confines of her automobile. She knew his hand rested less than an inch from her shoulder, and that with one quick move he would be touching her.

"Even you admit that you need to be saved from making a horrible mistake by marrying a man you don't really want." Leah's life, personal or otherwise, was none of his business. He admitted that fact, but it didn't change his determination to make her see the stupidity of her plan to marry just for the sake of marrying. A woman as lovely and intelligent and caring as Leah Marshall didn't have to settle for less than the real thing.

"You already know my life story—"

"Myrtle Mae didn't tell me everything," he said.

Leah took a deep breath, then glanced at Judd. He was staring at her intently. "I was ten when Daddy married Gloria. Larry was born a year later, then Lisa two years after that. Gloria was a lousy mother. As a matter of fact she was pretty much worthless as a person. I was already acting as a substitute mother for my brother and sister long before Daddy died and Gloria ran off."

"Yeah, my parents divorced when I was twelve. My mother took as much money from the old man as she could get and cut out." Judd glanced through the windshield. Ahead he saw tall pines and bushy cedars mixed and mingled with old oaks and towering cottonwoods.

"I'm sorry. Believe me, I know how difficult it can be without a mother. Luckily, I had Aunt Myrt. But she's hardly an acceptable role model for motherhood."

"Yeah, well, I wouldn't mind having an aunt like Myrtle Mae." Judd watched the road ahead. It seemed to go on

72 THE WANDERER

forever, twisting and turning as it changed from a paved road into a bumpy gravel lane. "She could have helped with my brother Jared. He was only three when our mother deserted us, and the old man wasn't good with kids."

"Your mother left a three-year-old child?" Leah wondered just how much Judd's mother and Gloria had in common. Two women who hadn't seemed to give a second thought to abandoning their small children.

"Yeah." Judd moved his hand, his fingers brushing Leah's shoulder. "I think Jared's birth was a last-ditch effort to save the marriage." Judd gripped her shoulder. "Why the hell they even tried, I'll never know. The only thing either of them ever cared about was money. He spent all his time making it, and she spent all her time blowing it. God, how that woman loved to buy things!"

"Where are your parents now?" Leah asked.

"Dead." Judd squeezed her shoulder tightly, then released her, allowing his arm to rest across the back of her seat when he edged closer to her. "The old man had a stroke. He died less than a year later. Her...she died of an overdose. Barbiturates and alcohol."

"I'm sorry."

"Yeah, me, too. But it happened a long time ago."

Leah turned the station wagon onto a dirt lane. "I want to show you something. Something very special to me."

Within minutes, she parked the car and opened her door. In the distance, Judd could see the burned-out remains of an old house. The brick chimney stood like a silent sentry guarding the land, waiting for rebirth.

"What's this?" Sliding across under the steering wheel, he got out of the car and stood behind her. He wanted to put his arms around her, to pull her back up against him.

"This belonged to my grandparents. Aunt Myrt and my mother lived here as children." Moving slowly, Leah walked forward. She well remembered all the stories her aunt had told her. Those stories were her only memories of her mother, who had died shortly after her birth. "As a matter

THE WANDERER

of fact, my great-great-grandfather built the house that once stood here. Before that, there was a log cabin built by my great-great-great grandparents.''

''Sounds like your family truly was a part of Tennessee history.'' Judd wondered what it would be like to be part of a family who could trace their roots back so many generations. In that way, Leah was like his ex-wife Carolyn, who knew the names of her ancestors who'd come from Europe.

''Marshallton was named for one of my ancestors.''

When she turned around, Judd looked at her and for one split second he couldn't breathe. She was so beautiful, standing there, with the sunlight casting a golden glow to her dark brown hair. He moved toward her, longing to reach out and capture the essence of purity and sweetness that radiated from her.

Leah could see the longing in his cinnamon eyes, those compelling eyes that were the exact shade of dark reddish brown as his hair and beard. He was looking at her as if he were some warrior lord who had just conquered the village and she was his virgin prize. ''I was engaged once. My father died two months before my wedding. Everything was set for me to graduate in May and marry in June.''

Judd stopped dead in his tracks. Why the hell was she telling him about some long-ago engagement? He didn't give a damn about the men in her past. He knew that, with a woman like Leah, there couldn't have been very many. She would never give herself to a man without love. He didn't know why he was so sure of that fact. Maybe because he was beginning to know Leah and to understand that there were women who could want a man for something besides his money. Leah Marshall just wanted a reliable, dependable man who could offer her marriage. ''What happened to your fiancé?''

''When Daddy died, we postponed the wedding.'' Leah turned around so she didn't have to face Judd. It had been a long time since she'd discussed her one great love affair

74 THE WANDERER

with anyone. She wasn't quite sure why she was telling Judd now. "Then after we'd set a new date, Gloria ran off, leaving me with Larry and Lisa. Terry just wasn't prepared to take on a ready-made family. I had to choose between him and my brother and sister."

Leah's shoulders trembled. Judd wondered if she was crying. He walked up behind her, put his arms around her and drew her back against his chest. "He never should have put you in that position. If he'd been any kind of man at all, he would have taken the kids."

Leah absorbed Judd's warmth and strength. She couldn't remember ever having someone to lean on, to give her support and care. "He . . . Terry wanted me to put Larry and Lisa in foster homes. And...and he wanted me to have Aunt Myrt committed."

"That bastard!" Judd lowered his head, rubbing the softly bristled side of his face against the smoothness of hers, nudging her neck with his nose. "He was a fool, honey. You're better off without him. And you're lucky you found that out before you married him instead of afterward."

"I guess you're right." Leah hadn't thought much about Terry in years. The last time she'd seen him, just before he and his wife moved to Kentucky, she'd cried herself to sleep that night. Terry had been her first and only lover. He'd been the sweet boy next door. Someone she'd known nearly all her life, the way she'd known Stanley Woolton.

"I know I'm right." Judd hesitated, uncertain how much of his past, if any, he wanted to share with Leah. "I married a woman for all the wrong reasons." He felt Leah tense. He tightened his hold about her, brushed a light kiss on her temple, then rested his chin atop her head. "Carolyn was young and beautiful and sexy. Her father and I . . . well, we went into business together." Leah didn't need to know that the chain of cheap motels he and Jared had inherited from their father was the beginnings of his vast empire, one that had doubled when he joined forces with David Cochran and

THE WANDERER

acquired the other man's hotels in downtown Memphis, Nashville, Birmingham and Jackson.

"You didn't love her?" Leah asked, wanting and yet not wanting to know the answer.

"Yeah, I guess I did, in a way." Judd ran his hands up and down Leah's arms. "Are you cold? The sun will be down soon."

"I'm fine," she said, shuddering. "Really, I'm not cold."

"Did you love this Terry?" Judd asked, and hoped she'd say no.

"Yes. I loved him."

"Do you still?"

"No, of course not." Leah could hear Aunt Myrt telling her that if Terry had been a grand passion instead of a youthful fling, that she would never have gotten over him, that she would never have stopped loving him. Undoubtedly Aunt Myrt had been right. What she'd felt for Terry had been similar, if not a little more intense, than what she felt for Stanley Woolton. "Do you still love your ex-wife?"

"I don't think I loved her after the first month. Once I stopped making love to her morning, noon and night, I realized there wasn't much of a person inside that sexy body and not much of a mind behind her big gray eyes."

Leah swallowed, her breath caught in her throat. She couldn't bear to think about Judd making love to his ex-wife. Images of his big body entwined with that of some beautiful woman flitted through Leah's mind. She squirmed to free herself from Judd's tenacious grip. "Let me go, please."

"No, don't walk away from me." He held fast, his lips moving across her temple, planting tender, frantic kisses. "I'm sorry I said that about Carolyn... about making love to her. I wouldn't want to hear about you and Terry."

"How long have you been divorced?" Leah hoped that it had been years and years. After all, her love affair had ended so long ago, she barely remembered what it had been like. She and Terry certainly hadn't made love morning, noon and night. As a matter of fact, they'd had sex only after their engagement, and the experiences had been less than memorable. Terry had made love to her with gentleness and care, but not once had he given her the intense kind of pleasure she'd read and heard about. Leah figured, for all intents and purposes, she was an oddball. At thirty-nine, she was a semi-virgin. Deflowered at twenty-one by her fiancé, who'd made love to her less than a dozen times and now she was seriously considering marrying a man who probably knew less about giving a woman physical pleasure than Terry had.

"Carolyn and I were married three years. We divorced when Steven was only a year old." Damn, why had he mentioned Steven. He hadn't meant to; the boy's name had just slipped out.

"You have a child?" For some reason, Leah didn't like the idea that not only had Carolyn been the lucky recipient of Judd's lustful passion, but she was the mother of his son.

"Did." Judd dropped his arms from around Leah. "Steven died three years ago."

Leah whirled around, catching Judd's big hand in hers. "What happened?"

"It was an accident." Judd wouldn't look at her. He knew she'd have tears in her eyes. Her tender heart would be bleeding for him, and he didn't want to face the pain he'd see reflected in her gaze. "I don't want to..." He cleared his throat, trying to dislodge the knot of anger and hurt that wouldn't go away. "I can't talk about it."

She opened her arms. Judd walked into her welcome embrace. She held him there, stroking his overlong hair with one hand as she rubbed his back with the other. "I've always dreamed of building a house here," she told him, her voice soft and tender. "I want a husband and a home. And I want a child."

She felt him stiffen in her arms. She understood that the loss of his son would always be a hurt inside Judd, a hurt that would probably never go away, despite time and dis-

THE WANDERER 77

tance. But he could have another child. She could give him a child. "I'm thirty-nine, Judd. I don't have much more time. Surely you must know what a child would mean to me."

He pulled away from her, grasping her by the shoulders. With a wild, almost desperate look in his eyes, he gazed down at her. "I don't want to get married again, Leah, but, if I ever do, I never want another child."

Searching his eyes for some sign of denial, Leah felt pinpricks of pain puncturing her heart. Surely he didn't mean what he'd said. The one thing on earth she wanted more than life itself was the one thing Judd Barnett said he never wanted. "I know another child couldn't replace the son you lost, but—"

"I will never father another child." His words were as cool and hurtful as the wintry breeze that had suddenly changed from warm to frigid. Leah shuddered.

Judd grasped her chin in his hand, still holding her shoulder with his other hand. "We're very different people. You want a stable relationship with a man you can count on for the long haul. You want that man to give you a child. I'm not that man. The only thing you want that I can give you is this." He lowered his head and kissed her.

At first she started to struggle, then stopped, admitting to herself that Judd was right. She did want this . . . this hard, thrusting kiss that took her breath away and made her knees weak.

He ran his hands over her, tenderly at first, then with harder, faster, more frantic need. "Do you know how much I want you? How many nights I've lain awake thinking about ripping your clothes off and burying myself deep inside you?" He nipped at her ear, his breath hot and damp.

"Judd . . ."

He clasped her hips in his hands, pulling her forward, letting her know the depth of his need, the strength of his longing. "I wonder what you'll look like naked and aroused." He glanced down at her breasts.

THE WANDERER

Her nipples instantly hardened. "Please don't...we can't...I..."

"Oh, honey, we can. All you have to do is say yes."

"No, I...oh, Judd don't do this to me."

"I'm tired of playing games. Tired of our watching each other with hungry eyes. Tired of wanting you so desperately that I ache with it."

Leah clung to him, breathless and hot, her heart hammering chaotically. She had never wanted anything so much in all her life. Judd wasn't the only one who'd wondered what it would be like between them. During the day she caught herself fantasizing about becoming Judd's lover. At night her dreams took on an erotic form, the very remembrance shocking to Leah's conscious mind.

"I want to touch you," he said, running his hands up to span her waist, his thumbs inching their way up her rib cage, then scraping back and forth beneath her breasts. "I want to hold you in my hands and taste you. I want to spread your legs apart and discover your secret heat."

Never had a man spoken to her the way Judd was doing. She had to stop him—stop him before she succumbed to his seduction. She couldn't deny that she wanted Judd to make love to her. The thought of the two of them making love sobered her instead of heating her passion. Judd Barnett was a wanderer, a man running from his past. He could give her temporary pleasure, perhaps even a grand passion, but soon he'd be gone and she'd be left with nothing but memories.

She went rigid in his arms. It took him a few minutes to realize that she had stopped responding to his fervent words and arousing touch. Judd rested his forehead against her, his breath harsh, ragged with unsated desire. "You want all or nothing, huh?"

"I'm sorry, Judd." Leah put her arms around his waist and gave him a comforting hug. "I do want you...more...more than I've ever wanted a man before."

THE WANDERER

79

He moved out of her embrace, putting several inches of cool air between their heated bodies. "But?"

"But I want more than an affair. More than . . . than . . ."

"More than a grand passion?"

Oh, dear Lord, why had he chosen that term? Aunt Myrt's words echoed in the stillness. Of course she wanted a grand passion. She had dreamed of having one for as long as she could remember. Why had the love of her life come along now, when time had run out for her? And why did she have to choose either the chance for marriage and a child of her own or an affair with the man she loved? Dammit, life wasn't fair. But why did that surprise her? She'd always known that she was one of those people who couldn't have it all.

"Yes, I want more than a grand passion. I've spent most of my adult life putting other people's needs and wants above my own." Leah sucked in a deep breath of chilly evening air. "You say that you never want to father another child, and maybe you don't. But even if you change your mind five or even ten years from now, it won't be too late for you."

"Leah..." When he reached out for her, she evaded him.

"You don't understand." She held out her hands in a pleading gesture. "I'm a woman who'll be forty in another year. Time isn't on my side."

He didn't try to touch her, but his gaze caressed her. The warmth in his eyes showed his tender concern. "I do understand about a woman's biological clock. What I don't understand is fate."

She stared at him, not comprehending the meaning of his words. He smiled, but there was no happiness in his expression, only a mirthless irony.

"Why did you and I meet now, when both of us have lived long enough and experienced enough that we know exactly what we do and do not want out of life?" he asked. "Unfortunately the only thing we both want is each other."

80 THE WANDERER

"I'm just not the kind of woman who can have a brief affair and walk away when it's over."

"I know," he said, taking her limp hand, bringing it to his lips for a gentle kiss. "But I'm going to stick around a few more weeks, that is, if I still have a job."

"You still have a job."

"Don't marry Woolton. Wait awhile longer." Judd released her hand. "Surely there's someone out there better for you."

You're better for me, her heart cried, but obviously he wasn't listening. "Stanley hasn't asked me to marry him, so there's no point speculating on—"

"How about going back to the shelter with me for a while tonight?" Judd asked. He didn't want to get into an argument with her about ol' Weasel Woolton. As long as he stayed in Marshallton, he intended to do everything within his power to discourage the other man's courtship.

"Why?" She hated to think that Judd was still staying at the Congregational church shelter. He no longer seemed like a shiftless bum to her. He was a man with a past, but little future, it seemed. And he was the man she loved.

"They fed a lot of people Christmas dinner today, and there's bound to be a big cleanup job. I'd like to go help out. To show my thanks to Reverend Brown."

"I certainly don't mind a little cleanup duty," Leah said. "Besides, I'd like to show my thanks to the reverend for being so kind to you and Taylor."

"Come on, then." Judd placed his hand in the small of her back and led her toward the old blue station wagon.

"You didn't have to see me home," Leah said as she unlocked the front door and entered the foyer. "Now, you'll have to walk all the way back to the shelter and it's nearly ten o'clock."

"I don't mind the walk. It's only a mile, and a good long walk should help me sleep better tonight." Judd followed her inside. "I wish we didn't have to say good-night."

THE WANDERER

"I've enjoyed being with you, talking to you, getting to know you a little better." Dropping her purse on a nearby table, Leah walked into the living room, noticing immediately that all the lights were still on. "Aunt Myrt? Aunt Myrt?"

"Maybe she's already gone to bed." Judd reached out to help Leah remove her coat. He laid it across the back of the sofa.

"Not Aunt Myrt. She's a night owl. She never goes to bed before midnight." Leah wondered if perhaps her aunt was having a late-night snack of leftover turkey.

His thoughts following a similar pattern, Judd said, "Maybe Taylor's still here and they're in the kitchen raiding the refrigerator."

Leah and Judd checked the kitchen. The light was out. "I don't understand this. Where could she be?"

"Calm down, honey, she's here somewhere." Judd wondered if when they found Myrtle Mae she'd be alone. "Maybe she and Taylor went out somewhere."

"Why would they have gone somewhere after she practically threw us out so that they could have the house to themselves?" Leah asked. "Something's wrong. I can feel it. Oh, Judd." She turned to him. "If anything has happened to her..."

Judd placed his arm around Leah's shoulder. "She's all right. She could be in her room, resting."

"Then why doesn't she answer me?" Leah pulled away from him and headed up the stairs, Judd directly behind her.

"Where are you going?" he asked.

"To see if she's in her room."

"Honey, I wouldn't do that—"

Leah swung open the door to Myrtle Mae's bedroom. One small crystal boudoir lamp lighted the room, casting pale lavender shadows across the white-and-brass bed where two people lay on top of the purple satin comforter. Myrtle Mae wore her purple-and-pink striped silk robe. Taylor's shirt was completely unbuttoned and the snap of his slacks undone.

"Oh, my God!" Leah covered her open mouth with her hand. She felt Judd's hard body stopping abruptly, shoving gently against her back.

"Just walk backward out of the room, close the door and pretend you didn't see a thing," Judd whispered in her ear.

"Aunt Myrt." Leah gulped, choking on her astonished outcry.

Myrtle Mae lifted her head off the purple satin pillow, her sleepy eyes trying to focus on her niece. "Leah, is that you?"

"Yes." Leah hated the squeaky tone of her voice.

"Go away," Myrt said, lying back down and snuggling up to Taylor, whose big arm came out to pull her closer.

"Aunt Myrt, what do you think you're doing?" Leah was well aware that her aunt hadn't lived a celibate life, but never, not once, had she brought a man home to her own bedroom. Surely this was a sign that Aunt Myrt had crossed that fine line over into complete insanity.

"I'm getting as much happiness out of life as I can." Myrt smiled at Taylor, running her fingers lovingly across his cheek before returning her attention to Leah. "We've been having the most wonderful time...talking. I guess we just fell asleep."

"Leah, let's go," Judd said.

"Is that you, Judd?" Myrt asked.

"Yes, ma'am, it's me."

"Oh, good," Myrt said. "Take Leah somewhere and show her what she's been missing."

It was all Judd could do to keep from laughing out loud. He only wished that Leah could see the humorous side of the situation.

"Myrtle Mae Derryberry, I demand that you—"

Placing his hand over her mouth, Judd dragged Leah out of her aunt's bedroom. Once they were in the hallway and

THE WANDERER 83

he'd closed the door, he released her. She turned on him, her blue eyes bright with anger.

"I want that man out of this house. What do they think they're doing? They're sixty years old. They're not married. They hardly know each other."

"Don't you think you're overreacting just a little? After all—"

"What do we know about Taylor? How can I be sure he isn't just using Aunt Myrt?" Leah covered her face with her open palms, shaking her head and groaning. "You simply don't understand. Aunt Myrt is like a child. She...she isn't quite normal. Mentally."

"Taylor loves her," Judd said. "He's told me that he does, and I believe him. He isn't going to hurt her."

"I hope you're right. Aunt Myrt is my responsibility, and if anything were to happen—"

"Is Stanley Woolton going to understand about Myrtle Mae? Or do you suppose he'll want to ship her off to the mental hospital?"

"What are you saying?"

"Have you and ol' Weasel ever discussed Myrtle Mae?"

"No, not really." She'd done everything she could to avoid any profound conversation with Stanley on the subject of her aunt.

"Don't you think you should?" Judd asked. "That is, if you're still planning on marrying the man, he deserves to know that you and Myrtle Mae are a package deal."

"Yes, you're right, of course." Leah walked slowly down the stairs, her head bent in defeat. Just before they reached the foyer, she turned abruptly and faced Judd. "If...if you were...I mean, if things were different and you were interested in marrying again, would you...that is, how would you feel about...about...?"

"If we were getting married, I'd consider Myrtle Mae a bonus. She's a special lady, and you're damned lucky to have her in your family."

Leah could feel the tears forming in her eyes. She wished them away, but they pooled in the corners and seeped down the sides of her face. Judd reached out and brushed them away with his rough fingertips.

Why, Lord, why couldn't Judd be the marrying kind? Leah wondered. I'd make him a good wife, and I'd give him a child. But Judd Barnett didn't want a child. He'd made that perfectly clear. He was the right man, but this was the wrong time and the wrong place. No matter how much she wished otherwise, her life and Judd's were headed in different directions.

Five

———

"So how are things coming along for the charity ball?" Pattie asked as she crossed out the original price on a Christmas tree ornament and marked the sale price.

"Don't ask." Leah threw up her hands in a sign of defeat. "Cora Woolton refuses to do anything differently from the way it's been done for the past hundred years. This charity ball is supposed to earn money for the local library, the children's little theater and The New Beginnings Society. Cora can't seem to get it through her head that we cannot spend huge amounts of money on this ball and still expect to make a profit."

"Well, you know my opinion of people like Mrs. Woolton," Pattie said, moving along the row of items on the New Year's sale table. "They're not really interested in helping anybody, just in making themselves look good. As long as the newspaper spells her name right and her club members give her their adoration, she could care less whether or not this project makes money."

86   THE WANDERER

"I hate to agree with you, you little liberal." Leah
laughed, then picked up a small box of Santa napkins and
placed the packs on the sale table. "I guess I've always
known that Cora and her friends were snobs. Lord knows
that you and Aunt Myrt have pointed it out to me on more
than one occasion."

"I'll bet she's still making some snide remarks about
Judd, isn't she?" Pattie asked.

Leah glanced toward the back storeroom, wondering if
Judd could overhear their conversation. "She's been upset
ever since she found out that Judd had Christmas dinner at
my house."

"I'll bet she's even more upset that you've let him move
in upstairs in the empty storeroom." Pattie squatted on her
knees in order to reach the bottom shelf of the sale table.

"She doesn't know."

With round, astonished eyes and an open mouth, Pattie
glanced up at Leah. "Uh-oh."

"It's none of her business."

"You're right," Pattie said.

"Judd needed a place to stay, didn't he?" Leah knelt
down beside her friend, lowering her voice so that there was
no chance of Judd overhearing them. "He couldn't stay on
at the shelter. And that room upstairs was empty except for
bits and pieces of junk and some boxes."

Pattie reached out, taking Leah's hand. "You don't have
to justify your actions to me. I like Judd, remember? I'm
one hundred percent in favor of you two getting together."

"We're not going to get together. Judd and I are friends.
He's my employee. That's all."

"He's an employee that you don't need now. Christmas
is over. It's mid-January and nobody is buying anything.
You could have let him go last week, but you didn't. And I
haven't heard you say anything about letting him go any
time in the near future." Pattie stood, dropped the black
marker into Leah's smock pocket and walked toward the
checkout counter.

THE WANDERER

Leah got up and followed Pattie. "All right, I'll admit that I don't want to see him leave Marshallton, and the only way to keep him here is to see that he has a job."

"Why don't you want him to leave?" Pattie picked up a bottle of glass cleaner and a dust rag from behind the counter.

"He's homeless," Leah said, reaching behind the counter to retrieve a feather duster. "If he leaves here, he'll be on the streets again. It's the dead of winter. I can't bear the thought of him being out there alone, hungry, and without a warm place to stay."

Pattie cleaned the glass counter. Spray. Wipe. Spray. Wipe. "Admit it, you care about him or you wouldn't be so worried."

"Yes, I care about him. I care too much, more than I should." Leah moved hurriedly away from her friend, moving the feather duster rapidly over nearby shelves.

Pattie set the glass cleaner down on the counter, dropping the dust rag beside it. "Why are you going to the charity ball with Stanley?"

"Stanley and I are still dating."

"You could ask Judd to be your escort."

"Don't keep doing this, Pattie." Leah continued moving along the shelves, flicking the feather duster up and down, back and forth, at breakneck speed. "Judd and I understand each other. I want marriage, a child and a stable life. Judd is a wanderer who doesn't want to get married and never wants to father a child."

"People change their minds, you know," Pattie said.

Leah stopped, turned around and faced Pattie. "And how long do you think it will take Judd to change his mind? A year? Two years? Ten? I don't have that long."

"So you're willing to settle for Weasel Woolton?" Pattie shook her head and grunted.

The front door opened. Leah and Pattie looked around, preparing to greet a customer. Instead they saw Lieutenant McMillian.

88   THE WANDERER

"Morning, ladies. Fine day if it wasn't so darn cold."
Mac removed his cap as he approached Leah.

"What can we do for you, Mac?" Leah asked.

"Well, Miss Leah, I sure do hate to bother you with this,
but...well...it's my duty." Mac looked down at his feet,
then glanced back up at Leah and frowned.

"What is it?" she asked.

"You still got that Barnett fellow working here?" Mac
asked.

"Yes." Cold dread spread quickly through Leah's body.
She felt her heart hammering away, issuing a warning.

"Well, I need to ask him a few questions. Is he here?"

"He's in back," Leah said. "I'll...I'll go get him."

"I could just go on back there with you and question
him," Mac said as he followed her. "That way, folks passing by won't see and wonder what's going on."

"Yes, thank you. That's a good idea."

Leaving a wide-eyed Pattie at the checkout counter, Leah
led Lieutenant McMillian to the back storeroom. Opening
the door, she saw Judd dumping trash into a large plastic
bag.

Judd turned around, smiling when he saw Leah. Then he
noticed the policeman following her. What the hell was
McMillian doing here? Had the officer come to harass him
again?

"Is something wrong, Leah?" Judd asked.

"Mac...Lieutenant McMillian wants to ask you some
questions."

"Yeah, what sort of questions?" Judd shoved the last
sack of trash into the plastic bag, twisted the top and closed
it with a tie.

"There's been another robbery. Third one since you came
to town, boy." Mac walked around Leah, who still stood in
the open doorway.

"So?" Judd turned his back on the officer, walking
across the room to open the back door.

THE WANDERER 89

A gush of cold January wind invaded the room. Leah shivered.

"Where do you think you're going, boy?" Mac hollered.

"I think I'm taking the trash out. Today's pickup day and the garbage truck will be here anytime now."

"Don't you go getting smart with me." Mac stomped across the storeroom, catching up with Judd in the alley.

Leah stood frozen to the spot, wanting to move but unable to get her feet to cooperate.

"What's going on?" Pattie asked, coming up behind Leah. "I could hear Mac's voice loud and clear out in the shop."

Leah jumped and cried out.

"Sorry," Pattie said. "I didn't mean to scare you."

"Mac thinks Judd is mixed up in the robberies we've been having in town the past few weeks."

"That's ridiculous," Pattie said.

Leah and Pattie walked together toward the back door, hesitating just before stepping over the threshold.

Mac placed his hand on Judd's shoulder. Judd dropped the huge plastic bag on top of the already-full Dumpster in the alley, then pulled away from the officer's hold.

"Look, I don't know anything about the robberies." Judd wondered just what he'd have to do to get this guy off his back. Why had good ol' Mac singled him out as the most likely suspect? Because he'd been a vagrant, someone new in town? Judd couldn't help but suspect that one of Marshallton's good citizens had suggested that Judd and Taylor could well be the thieves who had broken into several downtown businesses.

"Boy, you're trying my patience being such a smart aleck and not cooperating."

"And you're trying my patience," Judd said, "by continuing to call me boy."

Mac pointed his finger in Judd's face. "I'm going to be keeping close tabs on you, and if you so much as sneeze and

90   THE WANDERER

I don't like the sound, I'm going to be all over you. You got that, boy?'' Mac punched his finger into Judd's chest.

Judd looked down at the other man's hand, then back up into his face. Mac jerked his finger away and stepped back.

"I don't know who the hell you think you are," Judd said, his voice low, deep and even. "Wyatt Earp? Elliott Ness? Marshall Dillon? I don't care what part you're trying to play, Mac, but I should warn you that I'm not some ignorant bum you can keep harassing. I know my legal rights and, if you make it necessary, I can and will grind you into little pieces and feed you to the wolves."

Mac took several cautious steps backward, his hand resting atop his gun holster. Gulping hard, he cleared his throat. "You make one false move and I'll have you in jail." Mac brushed past Leah and Pattie, barely nodding on his way through the storeroom.

"Well, well," Pattie said. "Looks like our Mr. Barnett can take care of himself."

"Judd?" Leah rushed out into the alley, stopping so quickly that she almost fell into Judd.

"I don't know a damned thing about the robberies." He grabbed Leah by the shoulders. He could feel her trembling beneath his tense fingers.

"I believe you," Leah said, her warm breath creating white smoke as it mixed with the frigid air.

He'd never wanted to kiss a woman as badly as he wanted to kiss Leah right now. Without asking for any explanations or questioning him about an alibi, she'd said she believed him. He pulled her near, enveloping her shivering body in his embrace. Looking over the top of Leah's head, he saw Pattie standing in the doorway. Pattie smiled, nodded, then turned away.

"I need an hour off," Judd said, stroking Leah's back.

"Please don't—"

Judd cradled her chin in his hand. "I'm not going to cause any trouble. I just need to contact a friend who can help me."

THE WANDERER 91

Leah nodded agreement. Judd put his arm around her waist, leading her inside the storeroom. He slammed the door, jerked her into his arms and kissed her.

She felt like all the air had been knocked out of her lungs. His kiss was strong and wild and all-consuming. She clung to him, her slender fingers biting into his broad shoulders, pinching at the flannel material of his plaid shirt.

Judd could feel himself becoming aroused. Every time he touched Leah, he wanted her. But he could offer her nothing permanent, least of all the thing she wanted most. A child.

Breaking away, he gave her a slight shove. "I've got to go." He lifted his leather jacket from the metal hook on the wall, slipped into it and opened the back door.

"Take the station wagon," Leah said, then ran her tongue across her swollen lips.

"I can walk." He stepped outside and closed the door behind him.

Leah stood there, her eyes glazed over with tears. "Oh, Judd... Judd."

"He's quite a man, isn't he?" Coming up from behind, Pattie put her arm around Leah's shoulder.

"Yes, he is." Leah smiled at her friend.

"Why don't you invite him to go out with us for your birthday celebration this weekend? I could ask Fred and we could double-date."

Leah let out a deep sigh. "It won't work."

"What won't work?" Pattie asked.

"Judd and me. The chemistry is right, but everything else is wrong."

"Oh, Leah, do you have any idea what most people would give to experience that kind of chemistry?"

Tomorrow she would be thirty-nine. Tonight was supposed to be a carefree and frivolous celebration shared by Leah and her best friend. It wasn't that Pattie hadn't tried. Leah knew that it was her own fault that the evening had, so far, been less than memorable. But Leah wasn't the party-girl type that Pattie was, and except for agreeing to attend the rock concert at the local college, she simply hadn't been able to go along with any of Pattie's other ideas for painting the town red. Red was Pattie's color. Leah's was blue, a pale, cool blue.

"We'll order one round of drinks," Pattie said, practically shoving Leah through the door of The Country Pub. "If you feel uncomfortable after that, we'll leave."

"I hate bars." Leah wished she'd taken a deeper breath of fresh air while they'd been outside. "There's always so much smoke, and there's bound to be at least one obnoxious drunk."

"Gripe, gripe, gripe." Pattie nodded at the hostess when she held up two fingers indicating a table for two was available. "Come on. We've got a table."

On the small round stage to the left of the entrance, a band played dance music. A singer, young and handsome, with a dark, baritone voice, sang an old Nat King Cole standard, "Mona Lisa."

Pattie and Leah sat at the small table. A glass-encased white candle burned slowly, issuing a soft, romantic light.

"Relax, will you?" Pattie slipped off her fake-fur jacket, hanging it on the back of her chair. "Maybe we'll get lucky and a couple of gorgeous guys will ask us to dance."

"Lord, I hope not." Leah turned her attention to the waiter who'd just arrived. "Ginger ale, please."

"Oh, that's it, live dangerously." Pattie rolled her eyes heavenward, grunting. "I'll take a grasshopper."

"I'm sorry," Leah said. "I know this hasn't been a fun Saturday night for you."

"Don't be silly." Pattie glanced around the crowded room. "The concert was great. I just wish you'd enjoyed it more."

"I'm not much into rock music. That's more my style." Leah pointed toward the live band.

THE WANDERER 93

"Yeah, it's okay." Pattie continued her perusal of the lounge. "This place is nice, you know. Fred brings me here occasionally."

"I suppose it's the nicest bar in town." Although the room was sparingly lighted, creating a cozy, intimate atmosphere, Leah could tell that the lounge was beautifully decorated, stylish and clean.

"Hey, what else would you expect from a Southland Inns lounge?" Pattie asked, running her gaze up and down the bar. "This is where Taylor works, isn't it?"

"He's a desk clerk," Leah said. "He really likes the job, and he seems to be spending nearly all his money on showing Aunt Myrt a good time."

"And you were worried that he'd take advantage of her."

"I have to admit that he truly seems to care about her, but I still can't get used to their—" Leah lowered her voice to a whisper "—their affair."

"Get used to it." Pattie sucked in her breath.

"What's wrong?"

"Nothing. As I was saying about Aunt Myrt. She's happy. Taylor's happy. They're in love." Pattie couldn't seem to stop looking toward the bar.

Leah turned around enough to gain a clear view, "What's the matter with you? Who are you staring at? Oh, Lord, no."

Leah's gaze rested on Judd Barnett, sitting at the bar, a handsome, dark-haired man in a business suit at his side. The two seemed deep in conversation. Leah glared at Pattie.

"Don't look at me that way. I did not tell him that we'd be here tonight. Honest."

"Do you think he has a date?" Leah asked, praying that he didn't.

"He seems to be with that other guy," Pattie said. "I wonder who he is? He's awfully good-looking. Would you look at those shoulders, and that delicious cleft in his chin. What a gorgeous man."

94 THE WANDERER

The waiter placed paper coasters in front of them, then set down their drinks. Leah reached for her ginger ale. Tilting the glass to her lips, she gulped down the liquid. "As soon as we finish these, let's leave."

Pattie smiled. "Okay." Picking up her drink, she took a tiny sip.

Judd smiled back at Pattie Cornell. He'd had no idea that a trip to The Country Pub was part of Pattie's plans for Leah's birthday celebration. If he'd known, he would have made arrangements to meet Jared somewhere other than the lounge. But it was too late now. Pattie and Leah had already seen him, and they'd seen Jared, too. But there was no reason to think either of them would guess that Jared was his brother. Where both Judd and Jared had inherited their father's hulking frame, Judd had been blessed with his mother's auburn hair and brown eyes where Jared had taken after their black-haired, gray-eyed father.

"Are you going to tell me who this gift is for?" Jared asked, handing his brother a small, gold-foil-wrapped package.

"The lady in the back of the room. Five tables over. To the right." Judd glanced at Leah. She had turned her back to him.

"The blonde in the orange jumpsuit?" Jared asked. "She looks like one hot little number, big brother."

"Not her, idiot," Judd said. "The brunette sitting beside her."

"The one still wearing her coat?"

"Yeah, that's my uptight little Leah." Judd laughed, realizing that he did indeed think of Leah as his. If only she'd give in to her own desires, the two of them would be so good for each other.

"The woman you're working for?" Jared took a long look at Leah Marshall. "She's . . . different."

"Tomorrow is her birthday. Her aunt told me she hasn't been able to afford her favorite perfume in years. She raised

THE WANDERER 95

her younger brother and sister and put them through college.'' Judd fingered the white ribbon tied into a bow atop the small package.

"How are you going to explain being able to afford such an expensive present?''

"It's a small bottle.''

"A hundred-dollar bottle.''

"I'll tell her I borrowed the money from you—an old friend who owed me a favor.''

"If you're planning on giving it to her tonight, you'd better hurry,'' Jared said. "It looks like the lady is leaving.''

"What?'' Judd glanced over at Leah's table. She was standing and holding out Pattie's fur jacket. Pattie was still sitting. "Come on. I'll introduce you to Leah's friend.''

Judd slipped the tiny gift box into his shirt pocket, then got up and made his way across the crowded room. Jared followed.

Leah saw Judd the minute he stood up. Her heart raced wildly. Although not conventionally handsome, Judd was blatantly masculine, attractive in a ruggedly primitive way. Leah was sure that his earthiness piqued female interest wherever he went, and was, even now, teasing feminine senses throughout the room. She sat, hypnotized, unable to take her eyes off the big, bearded man who was walking toward her, his long, powerful legs striding purposefully in her direction.

Stopping at the edge of their table, he looked down at Leah. She stared up at him.

"Ladies,'' Jared Barnett said, in his most charming southern drawl.

Before Jared had a chance to say anything further, Judd held out his hand to Leah, who instantly stood and placed her small hand in his gigantic one. Judd slipped her coat off and tossed it on the chair.

96 THE WANDERER

"Well," Jared laughed, his gray eyes sparkling with amusement. "May I buy you another drink while our friends are dancing?"

"Sit down," Pattie said. "And, yes, thank you. I'd love another drink."

Leah had not been on a dance floor in years, and the last time she'd been dancing, she hadn't felt anything like this. Judd turned to her, holding out his arms. She stepped into them. He pulled her into a close embrace, fitting her body intimately against the long, hard length of his own. He was big and overwhelmingly powerful, yet he held her with a gentle possessiveness.

"I didn't know you'd be here tonight," he said.

"Coming here was Pattie's idea." Leah breathed in the heady aroma of Judd's clean male flesh.

"You two celebrating your birthday all alone?" Judd asked. "Where's Mr. Woolton?"

"Stanley's out of town on business."

"I suppose he'll be back in time to take you to the charity ball." Judd shifted her slight weight in his arms, positioning her as close to him as he possibly could.

Leah sucked in her breath. "Yes... the ball isn't for another two weeks."

"Don't go with him, Leah." Leaning low, Judd whispered in her ear. His breath was soft and warm. She shuddered.

"We agreed that nothing can happen between us. There's no future in our relationship." Leah clung to him, knowing if she let go, she'd fall, weak-kneed to the floor.

"You agreed," Judd said. "I didn't agree to anything."

"You know what I want." She gazed up into his glittering cinnamon eyes.

"And you know what I can give you."

With tears caught in her throat, Leah laid her head on his chest. They were at an impasse. They always would be as long as neither of them was willing to compromise.

Take 4 FREE Silhouette Special Editions

Plus

2 FREE gifts with no obligation

Special Editions bring you all the heartbreak and ecstasy of captivating and often complex relationships as they unfold today.

To introduce to you this powerful contemporary series we'll send you 4 Special Editions, a cuddly teddy bear plus a special mystery gift absolutely **FREE**.

We'll also reserve a subscription to our Reader Service for you which means that you could enjoy:

- ◆ 6 wonderful novels - sent direct to you each month.

- ◆ FREE Postage and Packing - we pay **all** the extras

- ◆ FREE Monthly Newsletter - packed with special offers, competitions, author news and much more.

Simply complete and return this card **today** to receive your free introductory gifts. There's no commitment - you may cancel your subscription at any time.

SEE OVERLEAF FOR DETAILS

FREE BOOKS AND GIFTS CLAIM

YES! Please send me 4 FREE Silhouette Special Editions together with my FREE teddy and mystery gift, without obligation.

Please also reserve a Reader Service subscription for me. If I decide to subscribe, I will receive 6 Special Editions for just £11.10 each month (subject to VAT), postage and packing FREE. If I decide not to subscribe I shall write to you within 10 days. The free books and gifts will be mine to keep in anycase. I understand that I am under no obligation - I may cancel or suspend my subscription at any time simply be writing to you. I am over 18 years of age.

Ms/Mrs/Miss/Mr _____ 7S3SE

Address _____

_____

_____ Postcode _____

Signature _____

mps
MAILING PREFERENCE SERVICE

NO
STAMP
NEEDED

Reader Service
FREEPOST
P.O. Box 236
Croydon
CR9 9EL

THE WANDERER

"It's probably just as well that I'm not the marrying kind," Judd said. "You wouldn't want to get stuck with a penniless drifter."

Still resting her head on his chest, she tilted her chin slightly and glanced up at him. He looked down and smiled.

"If I loved a man and he loved me enough to commit himself to me and a child for the rest of his life, it wouldn't matter whether or not he had a dime to his name." Leah lowered her gaze, settling it on the long, hairy column of his throat. "It would be nice to pay off all my bills and to never have to worry about my finances again, but nothing is as important as loving someone, least of all money."

Judd's steps faltered momentarily, but he quickly resumed his leisurely dancing, leading Leah slowly through the throng of couples, maneuvering her toward the darker side of the dance floor.

Why now, he asked himself, had he found a woman who honestly cared about him? A woman who had no idea that he was a multimillionaire who could give her the moon wrapped in a big red ribbon. He'd taken his father's prosperous business and doubled the family's meager fortune tenfold. All his life women had chased after him. He knew he wasn't a bad-looking man, but he was hardly the handsome type like Jared. Most of his women had liked his money more than they had him. Even Carolyn had married him as part of a smart business merger.

Judd thought that it was rather ironic that when he finally met a woman who cared for him only for himself, he wasn't in the position to accept what she was offering. She didn't want his money, which he would happily give her. She wanted a child...and he could never risk fathering another child and enduring the agony of losing it.

When he nestled the edge of his chin in her dark hair, her heavy eyelids opened and closed in dreamy confusion. She reached upward, resting her small hands on the solid width of his shoulders. While massaging the sensitive length of her neck with one hand, he moved his other hand downward,

98 THE WANDERER

pressing her hips into his hardness. Leah gasped silently on an indrawn breath when she felt the intimate contact of her soft, flat stomach with the solidity of his arousal. Instead of pulling away, she swayed closer, her short, tapered nails digging into the chambray material covering his shoulders.

Leaving his hand on her hip, he moved it ever so slowly to the rhythm created by her buttocks shifting back and forth to the beat of the music.

When the song ended, Judd held her close. She didn't try to leave his arms. The music began again. The young singer gave his own professional rendition of Percy Sledge's "When a Man Loves a Woman."

The song reminded them both of the first night they'd met—the moment they'd realized they wanted each other. Judd removed his chin from its resting place in her hair. Gripping her neck with his hand, he pulled her head slightly backward, just enough to enable him to see the warm, rosy flush on her beautiful face. Her skin was flawless. Her small, pink mouth was full and luscious, and her tiny nose fit perfectly beneath a pair of dark blue eyes that were gazing up at him, passing an age-old message of her feminine yearnings from her eyes to his. He leaned down, moving his mouth across her forehead, planting hot, quick kisses in rapid succession.

She wanted him to kiss her more than she had ever wanted anything in her life. She strained her face upward, encouraging his lips to join hers. Still holding her neck in his grasp, he pushed her mouth into his with a raging intensity that had her clinging to him for dear life. His lips consumed hers in their fiery conquest, her captive mouth surrendering to the passionate onslaught by opening for his invasion. He lunged his tongue into her softness, driving deeper and harder until she moaned, instinctively rubbing herself against him.

Reluctantly he pulled his mouth from hers, resting it against her ear. "Come on, let's get out of here."

For one brief moment, she was ready to go with him—anywhere. But the reality of her surroundings and what she was about to do struck her the moment she stepped out of his arms. "No, Judd. I...we..."

"Then let's find a table," he said. "Let's just sit and talk. Don't leave me, yet."

She gazed up at him. She'd never seen a man look at her that way before. As if he'd die without her. "All right. Let's...let's find a table."

They found a table that the busboy was clearing. Judd pulled out her chair; Leah sat, her spine stiff, her hands folded in her lap.

Judd sat, then motioned for the waiter. "Champagne?" He glanced at Leah, seeking her approval.

"Oh, my...no." She knew that Judd couldn't afford champagne. Why was he making such a suggestion? Surely he knew that he didn't have to impress her.

"What then?" he asked, reminding himself that he'd made a mistake by automatically ordering champagne to celebrate her birthday. No doubt, she was worrying about how he'd pay for it.

"Ginger ale, please." She forced a smile when she looked at the waiter.

"Make that two ginger ales," Judd said, then turned to face Leah. "You don't drink?"

"Not much." After nervously wetting her lips with the tip of her tongue, Leah bit down on her bottom lip.

"Well, I guess ginger ale is the best nonalcoholic celebration beverage." Judd reached inside his shirt pocket.

"What are we celebrating?" Leah's eyes widened in surprise when she saw Judd retrieving a tiny box from his pocket. He handed it to her. "For me?"

"Happy birthday, Leah." When she made no move to take the gift, he laid it down on the table in front of her. "I'd planned to bring it by your house tomorrow, since tomorrow is your birthday, but...since we ran into each other tonight..."

"Oh, Judd, you shouldn't have."

"Aren't you going to open it?"

100   THE WANDERER

Reaching out with shaky hands, Leah fingered the white bow. "It's wrapped so beautifully that I hate to open it."

"I hope you like it," Judd said. "Myrtle Mae gave me the idea. It's something she said you loved, but hadn't had in a long time."

Taking meticulous care not to damage the ribbon or the wrapping paper, Leah opened her gift. She held the tiny box in the palm of her hand. Tears gathered in her eyes. "Oh, Judd, you have to take it back. You can't afford this."

"Don't you like it?" he asked. "Myrtle Mae said it was your favorite. Joy perfume. Right?"

"Where did you get the money?"

"I didn't steal it." God, surely she didn't believe he was the thief who'd been breaking into the downtown stores lately. He'd never once thought that giving her this little gift might make her question his honesty.

"Of course I know you didn't steal it." She reached out, pulling his hand into hers and giving it a reassuring squeeze. "I only pay you minimum wage. You have to buy your groceries and...and you insisted on giving me rent to sleep in the upstairs storeroom. I'd hoped you were saving anything left over for the future, when...when..." Tears choked off the rest of her words.

He couldn't bear to see her crying over him, worrying about him as no one ever had. "Don't, Leah. I want you to take the gift and enjoy it, and don't worry about how much it cost." When he saw her looking at him with such tender compassion and genuine love in her eyes, he thought he'd die from wanting her. He encompassed both of her hands in his, the bottle of perfume nestled inside her grasp. "I borrowed the money from my friend Jared," Judd told her. "He's in town on business and I ran into him. He's owed me a favor for a long time."

"Thank you, Judd. I'll think of you every time I wear the perfume." At least a dozen questions flashed through Leah's mind—things she wanted to know about Judd, his past life and the people who'd been important to him. But

THE WANDERER 101

she knew he wasn't about to tell her anything until he was good and ready. Judd Barnett was a man with secrets, and Leah loved him enough to respect his privacy, even if it meant she'd never truly understand him.

"Mind if we join you two?" Pattie asked as she sat beside Leah.

Jared pulled an empty chair from another table and drew it up beside Judd. "Pattie and I were talking about driving up to Memphis for a little all-night fun. You two interested?"

"Hey, Judd, your friend is one super guy. He said y'all have known each other since you were kids." Pattie scooted her chair closer to Jared's and draped her arm through his. "This guy is rich, aren't you, sugar? He's got a limo outside waiting on him."

Judd glanced at Leah, catching the puzzlement in her eyes. She was probably wondering how Judd Barnett, a penniless drifter, could be friends with a guy wealthy enough to have a chauffeured limo.

"Your boss is a generous man, letting you borrow his limo," Judd said.

Jared laughed, deepening the cleft in his square chin. "Yeah, you're right. I'm lucky. The guy treats me like a brother."

"Did you meet Judd in school?" Leah asked. "Or were your families friends?"

Judd shifted nervously in his chair, glancing back and forth from Jared to Leah. He'd kill his brother if he said the wrong thing.

"Our families were friends." Jared cleared his throat. "Good friends."

"Well, hello, Ms. Marshall," Trey Woolton said as he came to a staggering halt beside the table, two other teenagers behind him. "I thought that was you I saw out on the dance floor a while ago, but I told myself it couldn't be. Why, Ms. Marshall wouldn't be rubbing herself all over some bum, practically doing *it* in front of everybody."

102   THE WANDERER

Both of Trey's friends laughed. Leah placed her hand atop Judd's, pleading silently with him not to lose his temper with these boys.

"I'm celebrating my birthday with my friends, Trey," Leah said calmly. "What are you doing in a lounge? You're only seventeen. Your father will be very upset and so will your grandmother."

"We came here to check out the action," a tall, freckle-faced boy said. "We picked up some beer over at Tango's and came by here looking for babes."

"Yeah, and it looks like this is the place to find some hot women," the other boy, a short stocky blond, said. "Why don't you two dump these old guys and let us show you a good time?"

"Why don't you three get the hell out of here," Judd said, "before I call the bouncer and have you thrown out."

"Nobody in this town would lay a hand on me." Trey got down in Judd's face, his sour breath reeking of alcohol. "Everybody knows how important my family is. I'm Stanley Woolton III, and I do whatever I damn well please."

Judd turned his head, glaring at Trey. "Well, I'm not from around here, little boy, and I could care less who you are or who your old man is. If you don't get your stinking mouth out of my face, I'm going to blister your backside."

Trey backed off. He grinned at his buddies and snickered, the sound an unsteady show of bravado. He turned again to Leah. "My daddy is going to be very upset when I tell him that I saw you kissing ol' scumbag here. And grandmother..." Trey doubled over with laughter, his slender young body swaying back and forth like a willow tree in a strong breeze. "Grandmother will not approve."

"Have all of you been drinking?" Leah asked. "Is there one of you sober enough to drive home?"

"I'll call Mac," Pattie said, leaning over to whisper to Leah. "I suggest we all get out of here before he comes to get these young fools. We wouldn't want Mac and Judd to lock horns again." Pattie excused herself.

THE WANDERER 103

Trey dug his car keys out of his pocket and dangled them in front of his eyes. "I drove. Don't worry about me, Ms. Leah Marshall. You worry about yourself."

Trey draped his arm around the short stocky blond and the three boys headed for the exit.

"Pattie's gone to call Mac," Leah said. "He's on duty tonight. It won't take him long to get here. I suggest we say good-night and all go our separate ways before he arrives."

Pattie came back to the table carrying her fur jacket and Leah's coat. "Mac's coming right over."

Leah turned to Judd. "I'll see you at work Monday." She picked up her present, slipped it into her purse and mouthed the words *thank you*.

He nodded, then watched her turn around and walk away.

"Why does Leah want us to leave before this Mac person gets here?" Jared asked.

"Mac is the police lieutenant who's been on my case," Judd said. "I think Leah's afraid I'll wind up in jail for assaulting an officer if Mac and I cross paths again."

"Then let's go up to my room, and I'll fill you in on what's going on at home."

"I don't want to hear anything about the problems you're having with Bess. They're your own fault." Judd found it hard to believe that the sweet little girl who'd once been his sister-in-law had become the business barracuda Jared accused her of being.

"Then let's talk about Leah Marshall."

"Let's don't."

"You're in love with her, aren't you?" Jared asked. "And she's in love with you, big brother. You, not your money."

"Leah deserves a lot more than I can give her." Judd walked toward the exit.

Jared moved faster, keeping in step. "Hell, man, you can give her everything money can buy."

"She wants a baby." Judd shoved open the swinging doors leading out into the lobby of Southland Inn.

104   **THE WANDERER**

Jared placed a restraining hand on his brother's shoulder. "You know what I think?"

"No, what do you think?" Judd glowered at Jared.

"I think that Leah Marshall is probably your last chance for love and happiness. If you haven't got the guts to accept what she's offering, then I doubt you'll ever return to the human race."

Six

"I hope you don't mind that I invited Judd to supper tonight," Myrt said as she laid the china plate on the dining table. "You know he told Taylor that he's planning on leaving town soon."

Myrt glanced over at Leah, who made no reply as she placed the white linen napkins by each plate, then reached out and picked up the silverware from atop the mahogany buffet.

After setting down the fourth dinner plate, Myrt idly fingered the arrangement of carnations and daisies Leah had used as a centerpiece. "Everything looks just lovely. But then, you have such excellent taste. So much like Mama." Myrt looked at the tall white candles perched in brass holders, one on each side of the flower bowl. "You must get tired of hearing me tell you how much you remind me of your grandmother."

Leah turned, opened the top drawer of the buffet and retrieved a small box of matches. When she slid the drawer

106 THE WANDERER

closed, she gazed into the rectangular mahogany-framed mirror in front of her. Reflections of a brass candelabra, a lace-covered table, and a Victoria étagère, filled with family heirlooms, blended into the background. Leah's own pale face stared back at her.

"Don't be silly, Aunt Myrt," Leah said, turning quickly, avoiding the reality of how the news of Judd's departure plans had affected her. "I'm honored that you think I take after Grandma Derryberry."

"Mama and Papa were madly in love, you know." Myrt closed her eyes, sighing loudly. "Their families were opposed to the marriage. He was Baptist and she was Methodist."

Leah couldn't stop herself from smiling. She'd heard this story before, many times, and she knew that Aunt Myrt was reminding her of it tonight for a reason.

Judd Barnett was the reason. "So they both joined the Congregational Church and lived happily ever after." Leah struck a match and lighted the candles.

"Compromises can be made in any relationship," Myrt said. "In fact, that's the only way most people make a relationship work. Surely you and Judd could—"

"How do you compromise about getting married and having a child?" Leah asked. "I want both. Judd wants neither."

"There are ways around that." Myrt gave herself a quick appraisal in the mirror, wetting her lavender-tinted lips and fluffing her hair. "Get yourself pregnant and Judd will marry you. I guarantee."

"Oh, Lord." Groaning, Leah closed her eyes tightly and shook her head. Opening her eyes, she took a deep breath before turning to face her aunt. "That has to be one of the most ridiculous gems of wisdom you've ever uttered."

"It would solve your problem."

"I would never deliberately do that to any man, and certainly not to Judd." Leah reached out, taking Myrt gently by the shoulders. "He lost his only child. He can't bear the

THE WANDERER

thought of ever experiencing the heartache of losing another child. I...I don't agree with his reasoning, but I do understand it.''

"Then compromise your unbending principles and have an affair with Judd before you commit yourself to a life of boredom with Stanley."

"I...I..."

"Something sure smells good," Taylor said as he entered the dining room. "Is that roast beef I smell?"

With a forced smile on her face, Leah turned to greet their guest, but quickly lost the smile when she saw Judd standing in the doorway. "Yes, it's roast beef." She tried to pull her gaze away from Judd, but she couldn't. He stared at her, his eyes questioning, his stance uncertain.

"With baby carrots and potatoes, green peas, homemade rolls and a coconut pie for dessert." Myrt slipped her arm around Taylor's waist, giving him an affectionate squeeze. "Are you hungry, sugar lump?"

"Starved," Taylor said. "Leah's such a great cook, I always look forward to one of her delicious meals."

Judd stepped through the doorway, stopping behind the carved mahogany captain's chair at the head of the table. "Myrt and Taylor insisted I join y'all for supper tonight. I hope you don't mind."

"Of course not." Leah wanted to go to Judd, to put her arms around him and hug him with the same easy familiarity Myrt used with Taylor. But she couldn't. She and Judd were only friends—barely friends. They weren't lovers. "Supper's ready. All I have to do is put it on the table."

"You didn't have to fancy things up here in the dining room," Taylor said. "We could have eaten in the kitchen."

"Oh, you know our Leah. She likes to do things up fancy," Myrt said.

"Can I help you with anything?" Judd asked, grasping the back of the chair so tightly that his knuckles strained until they turned white.

108   THE WANDERER

She didn't want to be alone with him in the kitchen. During the past two weeks, she'd done everything she could to avoid being alone with him at work. "That's all right, Aunt Myrt can—"

"Oh, let Judd help." Myrt pulled out a chair and sat down. "It'll give Taylor and me a few moments alone."

Leah knew darn well what her aunt was trying to do, but short of being rude, she couldn't think of any way to avoid the inevitable. "Everything's in the oven keeping warm. All we need to do is place the serving dishes on a couple of trays."

"No problem," Judd said, releasing his tenacious hold on the chair. "I've worked in a couple of restaurants before. I think I can handle the job."

He followed her into the kitchen. Taylor had smelled the aroma of food. All Judd could smell was the sweet, honeyed scent of Leah and the faint, exotic fragrance of the perfume he'd given her for her birthday. He came up behind her as she bent over to open the oven. The sight of her well-rounded behind encased in soft beige corduroy slacks did evil things to his libido. He could feel himself becoming aroused. He couldn't ever remember wanting a woman as much as he wanted Leah. Day and night. Night and day. Endlessly.

One by one she set the dishes on two large serving trays, not once turning around, not once even acknowledging Judd's existence. She had to keep her mind on supper, on serving the meal, eating the meal, and cleaning up afterward. Otherwise she'd lose her mind.

As she lifted one of the trays from the counter, she felt Judd move up behind her. Her hands trembled. He walked around her, taking the tray. His fingers brushed hers ever so slightly. Warm, liquid heat filled her.

Swallowing hard, she glanced at him and wished that she hadn't. He was watching her, staring at her as if he wanted to say something. "Thanks. I'll . . . I'll get the other tray."

THE WANDERER 109

He stood back, allowing her to go through the door first. When they entered the dining room, Judd followed her lead, setting his tray on the buffet and helping her place the food-laden serving dishes on the table. Myrt and Taylor, seated across from each other, were laughing and smiling like a couple of young lovers.

An hour later, Leah couldn't remember what she'd eaten, let alone how much. Although she and Judd had both tried to participate in the lively conversation that Myrt and Taylor began, neither of them seemed in the mood for idle chitchat. The only bit of information Leah recalled was the discussion about the local robberies. Two more thefts had been committed, and Mac had questioned both Taylor and Judd, again warning them.

"We're going to take our coffee into the den and watch that comedy special that's coming on at seven-thirty," Myrt said. "Why don't you just leave this mess till morning and I'll put everything in the dishwasher?"

"You and Taylor go enjoy yourselves," Judd said as he stacked plates and serving dishes on a tray. "I'll help Leah clean up."

"That's not necessary." Leah shook her head, wanting to discourage Judd's assistance.

"Fine idea, my boy," Taylor said as he slipped his arm around Myrt and escorted her out of the dining room.

Silently Judd and Leah cleared away the dishes and carried the trays into the kitchen. Like two mute robots they went about the business of loading the dishwasher and straightening the kitchen. As they worked side by side, neither of them speaking, their glances occasionally locking, Leah and Judd made a concentrated effort to keep from touching each other.

When Leah hung the last stainless steel pot on the wall rack and opened the drain on the sink, Judd reached out and took her small, trembling hands into his large steady grasp.

She darted a quick look at him. He smiled, then took the towel he held and ever so slowly began to dry Leah's hands.

110   THE WANDERER

He took special care to run the soft terry towel over each finger, stroking the moisture from her flesh.

With the task complete, Judd ran his hands up Leah's arms in a cautious, gentle manner, stopping when he reached her shoulders. He pulled her toward him.

"You smell good." He nuzzled her neck, and thought he'd die when he heard the tiny gasp of sexual pleasure that escaped from her throat.

"It's your... your perfume." She closed her eyes, drinking in the sheer physical enjoyment of having him so near. How, she wondered, could one person possess so much power over another?

"My perfume on my woman." He gripped her shoulders tightly, with gentle strength.

"Judd, please don't."

"Don't what?" he asked, whispering the words in her ear. "Don't talk to you? Don't touch you? Don't want you?"

"Don't do this to me. You know how I feel...what... what I want." She jerked away from him, desperate to remain in control of herself, her emotions and her actions.

Judd stared at her, wondering exactly what it was about this one particular woman that had his head spinning and his male hormones doing the riot act. She was lovely; that was a fact. But the world was filled with attractive women, and most more available than Leah. Was it her face or her hourglass-shaped feminine body? Was it the way she walked or talked? Was it the sound of her laughter? Or was it the goodness in her heart? Perhaps it was all those things. He didn't know.

"Why does it have to be all or nothing with you?" He took a step toward her, then stopped when she backed away.

"I'm too old to settle for anything less," she said. "My best years are going fast."

"Dammit, you're only thirty-nine, not ninety-nine."

When he walked toward her, she edged her way backward and up against the wall. His big body hovered over

THE WANDERER

her, only inches separating them. She looked at him, silently pleading for his understanding. He didn't say a word. He didn't touch her. Leah knew he was holding himself in check, using his willpower to refrain from doing what he wanted to do—what she really wanted him to do.

Judd was such a powerful man. In faded jeans that clung to his slim hips and muscular legs, and a plaid flannel shirt that couldn't disguise the width of his massive shoulders, he epitomized masculine strength.

"Aunt Myrt said that you told Taylor you planned to leave Marshallton soon. Is that true?" She held her breath, not wanting to hear his reply.

He leaned into her. Her lips almost touched the top button of his shirt, her nose grazing his thick, auburn chest hair at the point where it reached his neck.

"You don't really need me at Country Class, and we both know it," he said, then buried his lips in her hair.

"Where...where will you go?" Her knees trembled, weakening more and more as he mouthed her hair along the side of her face.

"Wherever the road leads. On to the next town. It really doesn't make any difference to me." Releasing her shoulders, he reached out, running his fingertips over her cheek while his lips spread a series of delicate kisses across her forehead.

"Don't go. Stay here." She couldn't bear the thought of his leaving, of never seeing him again.

"I can't stay." His lips moved downward, brushing against hers. "I lie awake at night wanting. Every day at the shop, I walk around with an arousal. And I know you're as hot for me. I can see it in your eyes every time you look at me."

She wanted to deny his statement, but she couldn't. He was right. "Stay. Stay a few more weeks. Until the end of February. Maybe...maybe..."

112   THE WANDERER

"Maybe one of us will give in, change our mind?" He opened his mouth over hers, sucking in the smell and taste of the woman he longed to possess.

"It's possible." She spoke the words into his open mouth. "Anything's possible."

"One more month?" he asked.

"If you stay here, at least you'll have a place to sleep and food and a little money." Images of Judd huddled on a park bench and covered with newspapers flashed through Leah's mind. She slipped her arms around his waist, hugging him with loving concern. "You don't know how much I want to take care of you."

Her words touched his heart. He could never remember a time in his life when someone had wanted to take care of him. Not even his own mother, and certainly not his spoiled, selfish wife.

He'd hoped that Leah had expended all her motherly instincts on raising her brother and sister, but obviously a woman like Leah had more nurturing love to give. She wanted to give it to him. And, dear God, he wanted to take it. He wanted to lose himself in her loving arms, in the gentle giving sweetness that was Leah. But she wanted more than Judd. She wanted his child. He closed his eyes and shuddered. He could imagine what Leah would look like, her belly swollen with his child. In his mind, he could clearly see her holding a babe to her breast. The image filled him with happiness and peace. But in the dark, guilt-ridden recesses of his memory, lay the image of Steven's small, lifeless body resting inside his bronze coffin.

Feeling his withdrawal, she held him, trying to absorb some of his pain, knowing that he was reliving a memory he could not yet share with her. "I'm here, Judd. I'm here."

He grasped her fiercely, as if nothing and no one mattered but her. His mouth took hers, greedily sipping, hungrily consuming the loving comfort she gave him.

He pulled away from her, holding her at arm's length. Breathing heavily, he framed her face with his hands. "I'll

THE WANDERER 113

stay. For a while.'' When she started to speak, he covered her lips with his thumb. ''I'll stay because I want you, and heaven help me, I need you.''

''Oh, Judd, I want—''

''But don't think that time is going to change the way I feel.'' He gazed into her teary eyes and wished that he had the strength to give her what she wanted, to fulfill her dreams. ''I will not ever father another child. I don't deserve the right to be a parent. When I had the chance, I failed miserably at the job and my son paid the price.''

''We all deserve one last chance at happiness. I do, and...and you do.'' Leah couldn't stop her tears from escaping, although she tried. Sucking her breath in deeply, she willed herself to be strong. But her tears ran down her cheeks and fell onto Judd's hands.

''You deserve far more than I can give you.'' He kissed the tears from her cheeks, savoring the salty taste of her sadness, a bittersweet part of his Leah.

''What I deserve is you.''

He released her and stepped away. ''Then take me to the charity ball,'' he said.

''What?'' She looked at him, stunned by his request.

''If I'm who you want, then stop seeing Stanley. Don't go with him to the charity ball tomorrow night.''

''But...but we've already made plans. I can't break our date at the last minute like this. It wouldn't be fair to Stanley.''

''It isn't fair to Stanley to lead him on when you don't want him.''

''I...I...'' Confusion confronted her on all sides. She wanted Judd, but he wouldn't offer her marriage or children. She didn't want Stanley, but she knew it was only a matter of time before he proposed, and he'd made it perfectly clear that he longed to have more children.

''It's still all or nothing, isn't it?'' Judd shook his head. ''We're in a no-win situation, honey.''

114   THE WANDERER

When he turned to leave, she grabbed him by the arm.
"Don't leave Marshallton. Please."

He looked down at her hand where it gripped his sleeve.
"I'll stick around...for a while." He pulled away from her,
walked to the door, stopped and turned around. "After all,
anything's possible. Right?" He shoved open the kitchen
door and walked out into the hall.

Leah didn't follow him. She knew they couldn't settle
anything tonight. Tomorrow evening she'd attend the charity ball with Stanley and try her best to find him attractive.
When he brought her home after the ball, she could invite
him in and they could build a fire in the fireplace. And
maybe, just maybe, Stanley's kisses would ignite some small
flame of desire within her. She reluctantly admitted that she
could never expect the raging inferno of longing that Judd
created inside her. But, if she tried, it was possible that she
could learn to want Stanley, a reliable man who was ready
to settle down and raise a family.

He'd been watching her like a hawk all day. She didn't
know how much more she could stand. When he'd come
down from the storeroom this morning, the first thing he'd
asked was if she still planned to go to the charity ball with
Stanley. When she'd said yes, he hadn't replied. He simply
nodded his head and walked away. Although he'd pre-
tended to ignore her, not speaking to her except when she
spoke to him first, he'd been staring at her for hours and
hours.

She looked out the storefront window. Judd was sweeping the sidewalk where a blustery February wind had scat-
tered trash and dust and dead leaves. He glanced at her.
When she smiled, he looked away.

The front door swung open and Pattie came rushing inside. Twirling around and around, she flung out her arms
and stopped directly in front of Leah.

"Well, how do I look? Do you like my hair? Sophisti-
cated, huh?"

THE WANDERER 115

"It looks wonderful." Leah could never remember Pattie's hair being so subduedly styled, but the sleek, slicked-back coiffure did give her friend an air of elegance.

Pattie hugged Leah. "Thanks for letting me have the time off to drive into Jackson. Tony Sanders is simply a genius, and I couldn't let just anybody do my hair for tonight."

"Of course not." Leah wished that she felt half as exuberant about tonight's big shindig as Pattie did.

"I've never been to the country club before. Fred's a member, you know."

"How serious are you about Fred?" Leah asked.

"If he asked, I might marry him."

"Wow. I had no idea. I guess I thought you enjoyed being single too much to settle down."

"You forget, old friend. I, too, have a biological clock that's ticking away." Pattie went into the back storeroom to hang up her jacket. Calling out rather loudly, she said, "But I happen to love Fred, and we're dynamite in bed together."

Judd came in just in time to hear the last of Pattie's declaration. Leah glanced at him. He glared at her, not speaking and yet his look expressing far more eloquently than words ever could have exactly what he was feeling. Leah knew that he was telling her that, if she'd give them the chance, the two of them would be dynamite in bed together.

"Oh, hi, Judd," Pattie said as she came out of the storeroom. "Listen, I think you should know that Mac questioned me about your comings and goings today when Fred and I were having lunch over at The Barbecued Pig. He's determined to pin these burglaries on you."

"Yeah, I know." Judd walked past Leah, heading for the storeroom. "Don't worry about it. He can't arrest me without evidence, and there isn't any."

Pattie slipped behind the front counter beside Leah who had opened the register and was dumping out a fresh roll of quarters. "Go talk to him."

116   THE WANDERER

"Why?" Leah asked.

"Fred told me that Trey Woolton is the one who's keeping a fire lit under Mac about Judd being the burglar who's broken into all the stores. Trey pointed out that it's strange that Country Class hasn't had a theft when two stores on this block have."

"What interest would Trey have in pointing a finger at Judd?"

"Maybe his daddy put him up to it."

"Stanley wouldn't do such a thing." Leah slammed shut the cash register. "Besides, he'd have no reason."

"How about jealousy?"

"Stanley doesn't consider Judd a threat to our relationship."

"I think you should tell Judd about Trey. That boy is up to no good, I can tell you that," Pattie said.

"All right." Leah checked the time on her wristwatch. "It's almost closing time—"

"I'll take care of things up here." Pattie shooed Leah away with a sweep of her hands. "Go on."

Leah opened the closed storeroom door. Judd had his back to her, but she knew he'd heard her enter. He stood rigid and unmoving.

"Judd?"

He didn't turn around. "Yeah."

"Word has it that Trey Woolton is convinced you're the burglar the police are looking for, and... and he's bad-mouthing you to Mac."

"I'm not surprised."

"Stanley probably doesn't know anything about what Trey is doing."

Judd turned, his gaze locking with hers. "Do you think Stanley is too much of a gentleman to fight dirty?"

"Yes."

"Stanley is a gentleman. A reliable, steadfast man." Judd walked toward Leah. "He's a solid citizen with a nice fat bank account. He can solve all your problems, can't he?"

THE WANDERER 117

Leah backed up against the closed storeroom door. Judd stopped, placed his hands on both sides of Leah's head and leaned downward.

"Stanley can get you out of debt. He can offer you marriage. And he wants children. That's everything you want, isn't it, Leah?"

"Don't..." Hot pink stained her cheeks, and warm quivering tremors racked her stomach.

"Money, marriage, children. What more could you want?" He pressed himself against her. "When you marry him and live in his fine house and sleep in his bed, you'll remember me. You'll think of this." He dragged her up against him, urging the cleft of her soft body into the hardness of his.

She gasped. He took her mouth in a hungry kiss, a kiss meant to dominate her. She couldn't stop herself from responding, her body reaching out for his, her femininity drawn to his masculinity.

He trailed a line of damp, passionate kisses from her lips to her chin and down her throat. He opened the top two buttons of her blouse and continued anointing her flesh with his mouth. She squirmed against him, knowing she should tell him to stop, knowing it was madness to allow him to continue. He covered her breast with his open mouth, suckling her through her blouse and bra.

Her nipple hardened instantly. She cried out, and clung to Judd. He raised his head and looked at her.

"You can go to the ball with Stanley and you'll wish you were with me. You can marry him, have sex with him, have his child, and you'll still want me."

Judd released her, and when she clung to him, he shoved her away. She watched, her mouth dry, her eyes filled with tears, as he grabbed his battered leather jacket off the wall hook, tossed it over his shoulder and walked out the back door into the alley.

Leah slumped against the wall. She ran her shaky fingers over her swollen mouth, then glanced down at her blouse.

118 THE WANDERER

A large, wet circle stained the area around her breast. Shudders of intense longing racked her body. She bent over double, hugging herself, screaming silently.

Judd stuck his hands in the pockets of his leather jacket, then marched in place trying to warm himself. The temperature had dropped steadily since the sun set nearly six hours ago, and the low, whining northeasterly wind ate through Judd's clothes like acid through metal.

Where the hell was she? He knew it was close to eleventhirty because he'd left the shop right at eleven and it took ten minutes to walk the few blocks from Country Class to Leah's home. Although he felt frozen enough to have been outside for hours, he knew it hadn't been longer than fifteen or twenty minutes.

He had called himself all kinds of a fool for being here. Any guy who'd hide in the bushes, waiting to see some other man bring his woman home from a date, had real trouble in the brains department. He'd told himself again and again that Leah wasn't going to do anything crazy like go to bed with Stanley Woolton. But he also knew that tonight would be the perfect night. Myrtle Mae wouldn't be home. She was staying with Taylor after the ball. Besides, Leah was probably hurt and angry with him, after the way he'd treated her this afternoon. He'd said some pretty rough things to her, so she might be upset enough to try to seduce another man to prove him wrong.

When he heard the sound of a car in the driveway, he peeped through the high shrubbery that ran the length of the drive and separated Leah's property from her neighbor's. The black Mercedes belonged to Woolton. Judd watched while Stanley got out, walked around the car and opened the door for Leah. The moment she put her hand into the other man's, Judd had to confront the urge to run out and jerk her away. Instead he remained silent, watching and waiting.

The creamy glow from the half moon assisted the muted illumination coming from the nearby streetlight. Judd could see clearly the midnight-blue luster of Leah's satin evening gown and matching shawl, the shimmery glitter of the rhinestone earrings she wore, and the moist softness of her rose-tinted lips. If she were his, truly his, she'd never wear rhinestones again. Diamonds and sapphires would adorn her ears and throat, not cheap imitations. If Leah were the kind of woman who longed for the things money could buy, Judd knew he would buy her the world. But Leah didn't want all the fancy things money could buy. She wasn't interested in the ephemeral, only in the everlasting.

When Leah unlocked her front door, she stepped inside. And Stanley Woolton followed. As soon as the door slammed shut, Judd walked out from behind the shrubbery, slowly making his way toward the window. Damn, he felt like the sneak thief Lieutenant McMillian thought he was. But he wasn't out to steal anything. All he intended to do was keep guard over what was his.

"Would you care for some coffee?" Leah asked as she led Stanley into the living room.

"A little white wine would be nice, don't you think?" Stanley removed his gloves, stuck them in the pocket of his coat and neatly laid the coat over the back of the wooden rocker by the window.

"I don't think I have any." Leah remembered that Aunt Myrt and Taylor had finished off the only bottle of wine in the house. "I'm sorry, but you know I seldom drink."

Stanley sat on the sofa, patting the seat beside him. "Forget the wine. Come sit down."

Leah let her shawl fall from her shoulders, but held the satin garment together at her waist. She sat down. Stanley put his arm around her and drew her close. He took her hand. "We could build a fire," she said.

"That would be a bit messy, wouldn't it? And you wouldn't want me to ruin my tuxedo."

"No, of course not."

120   THE WANDERER

"The ball was quite a success, wasn't it?" He brought her hand to his mouth and bestowed a gentle kiss on her knuckles.

Stanley was so nice, Leah thought. Polite and gentlemanly. "Oh, it was a huge success. Cora should be pleased."

"Mother was thrilled. She's so involved in charity work, and it pleases her that you take an active part in the social scene." Stanley leaned over, puckering his lips as he pulled Leah into his arms.

"I'm pleased that your mother is pleased." Leah leaned into the kiss, longing for feelings of ecstasy to sweep her away.

Stanley's mouth was soft and wet. His kiss was tender and surprisingly passionate. Leah flung her arms around his neck, drawing him closer. Her shawl fell onto the sofa. She ran her tongue over his lips. He groaned, and opened his mouth. Slipping her tongue inside, Leah deepened the kiss.

Something was wrong. Terribly wrong. She was kissing and being kissed with a great deal of enthusiasm, and yet all she could feel was the chill on her bare shoulders, the stickiness of Stanley's mouth, the overpowering odor of his expensive cologne.

She closed her eyes, hoping the feeling of uneasiness would go away and be replaced by one of desire. Leah ended the kiss by pulling away slightly, her arms still draped around Stanley's neck.

"My, my, Leah, that was some kiss."

She looked at Stanley. At his fogged glasses and his red cheeks. He looked rather adorable, but unfortunately he didn't look desirable.

A slight scratching noise on the far side of the room drew Leah's attention from Stanley to the window. She gasped aloud.

"Is something wrong?" Stanley asked.

"No, nothing," Leah said, her voice a shrill screech as she stared at Judd Barnett's face pressed against the pane. "But

THE WANDERER

it is late, and I'm very tired." Loosening her hold on Stanley, Leah stood.

Stanley stared up at her, a puzzled look in his black eyes. "Yes, I understand. But...but I had hoped that we could...could..."

"Another night," Leah said, trying to avoid staring at the window, yet unable to keep herself from checking again to make sure she wasn't seeing things. Judd Barnett was still there.

Stanley stood, picked up his coat from the chair and put it on. All the while Leah walked him to the door, she kept shifting her gaze backward toward the window. She prayed she could get Stanley out of the house and in his car before he saw Judd.

Leah opened the front door. Stanley leaned over, pulled her into his arms and gave her a rousing farewell kiss. "You're so beautiful, Leah. So beautiful you take my breath away."

Glancing over Stanley's shoulder, Leah saw Judd walking across the sidewalk toward the huge oak tree in the yard. "Call me soon."

"Sweet dreams, darling," Stanley said. "Dream of me." She waved goodbye when he backed onto the porch. "And you dream of me." She stayed in the open doorway until Stanley got in his car and drove out of the driveway.

The minute she started to close the door, Judd walked out from behind the oak tree. They exchanged glances. He headed for the porch. She started to slam the door, but before she got it shut, Judd stuck his foot over the threshold.

"Go away, Judd!" She leaned against the door, hoping the pressure was hurting his foot.

"If I do, will you dream of me?" His voice mocked Stanley's. "Does he babble that nonsense all the time?"

Leah flung the door open wide, and with her hands planted squarely on her hips, she glared at Judd. "Are you crazy? How dare you sneak around outside my house and peep in my windows!"

122 **THE WANDERER**

"How else was I going to know what you were doing with ol' Weasel Woolton?" Judd ran his hands up and down his arms. "It's cold out here, you know. I could freeze to death."

"It would serve you right."

"If you hadn't seen me in the window, would you have let Woolton spend the night?"

"That's none of your business."

"You two were practically making out on the couch. He would have stayed if you'd asked."

"I know that." She could feel the cold night wind swirling around her ankles, nipping at her bare shoulders and chilling her uncovered chest.

"Did he make you feel the way I do?"

"Go away, Judd."

He reached out, running the tip of his index finger down her throat and across her collarbone, stopping just before delving between her breasts. "Answer my question."

"No. He didn't make me feel the way you do." She swayed slightly toward Judd.

"I couldn't bear to see him touching you, kissing you." Judd jerked her into his arms, pulling her feet off the floor.

"I wanted to want him. I tried. I tried so hard." Leah accepted the inevitable, allowing Judd to lift her into his arms.

He looked at her. She looked at him. "I want to carry you inside and upstairs to your bedroom. I want to stay and spend the night making love to you."

"Judd..."

"Tell me you want me to stay."

"I want you to stay."

He carried her into the foyer, slamming the door shut with his foot.

Seven

The door to Leah's bedroom stood open invitingly as Judd carried her over the threshold. The pale glow from an antique brass-and-glass hurricane lamp created soft shadows that hugged the corners and caressed every object in the room. A glimmer of moonlight wafted through the sheer lace curtains, casting a dark reflection of the swaying branches of the willow tree that scraped the side of the house.

Leah clung to Judd, her arms draped around his neck, her head lying on his shoulder. Somewhere in the back of her mind a little voice warned her that this was wrong, that she would live to regret her decision to give herself to Judd. But her heart wasn't listening, and neither was her body. She loved this man, and she wanted him more than she'd ever wanted anything. Even more than she wanted a child.

When they entered her room, her very private domain that she'd never shared with another, Leah felt a sudden timidity and realized that it was a woman's ancient fear of being alone with the man who would soon possess her for the first time. Instinctively she squirmed in his arms.

Judd lowered her to her feet, gradually letting her slide down the length of his hard body.

"Oh." Leah could not refrain the gasp as she moved against his arousal.

"You know I want you." He reached out, grasping her shoulders. Slowly, gently, he ran his hands down her arms, crossing over to linger at the swell of her breasts. He circled the top of her bosom, exposed by her strapless gown. Untouched but yearning, her nipples stabbed into the blue satin bodice. Leah moaned and swayed toward him as he lowered his hands, making a steady but leisurely survey of her slim waist, her round hips, her firm behind and flat stomach.

"Judd..." She was hot for him. Wild and on fire—and he hadn't even touched her intimately.

He tugged at the side zipper of her dress, releasing it with one swift jerk. The top of her dark blue gown fell to her waist. His gaze covered her naked body.

"Perfect," he said as he ran the tip of his index finger down the cleft between her breasts.

Warmth spread through her like July sunshine across an asphalt street. "They're small."

He leaned over, tenderly kissing her shoulder. "Your breasts are perfect." He reached out and encompassed her, lifting her breasts. "They were made for me. See... a perfect fit."

Leah swallowed hard, awash with emotions so intense she could find no words to express them. She wanted to show Judd what she felt deep in her heart.

She slid her hands inside his jacket, easing it off his broad shoulders. It fell to the floor. She sought the buttons of his faded shirt, releasing them from their openings. Delving inside, she curled his thick russet-brown chest hair around her fingers. Swamped by desire, she glided her hands over every inch of his chest, pulling at his shirt until it came free

THE WANDERER 125

from his jeans. She raked her nails across the muscles in his back and, standing on tiptoe, buried her lips in the hollow of his throat. He lifted her off the floor. Her feet dangled in midair.

"Mmm...mmm..." The humming chant on her lips vibrated against his hot flesh as he lifted her into his arms once again. She moved her mouth in a frenzied exploration of his throat and shoulders. Covering his chest with wild, wet little kisses, she whisked her tongue across one nipple and then the other, savoring the salty sweet taste of his maleness.

"Leah, honey, do you know what you're doing to me?" He spoke the words in a low, hungry growl. In all his life, he had never wanted a woman this badly. For the first time since Steven's death, he was truly glad to be alive.

"What...what am I doing to you?" she asked, gazing into the depths of his cinnamon-brown eyes.

"You're driving me crazy, honey. I'm ready to explode."

Leah had never known the kind of erotic urges that Judd inspired. No other man had ever brought to life the passion buried deep within her. She couldn't believe how much she wanted him, how desperately she longed to belong to him, to love him and be loved in return. In some ways Judd was practically a stranger, and yet he wasn't. On some instinctive level, she knew that they were meant for each other, that Judd needed her in every way a man can need a woman. And tonight that was exactly what she would be—his woman.

"Judd," she whispered as he bent over, laying her down on the antique oak bed. "I want you to make love to me."

Standing over her, his gaze fixed on her breasts, he flung his shirt to the floor and unbuckled his leather belt. "I'm going to, Leah. I'm going to make love to you all night."

Leah's eyes grew wide with wonder and expectation. Her mouth opened on a sigh of pure pleasure and anticipation. Totally naked, Judd looked at her, desire in his eyes. She swallowed, then blinked several times. Filled with rioting emotions, she stared at him, at the magnificence of his big,

126 **THE WANDERER**

hard and undeniably aroused body. A sudden, innate fear surged through her, freezing her into lifeless immobility.

Judd sensed the change in her immediately. "I'm dying to be inside you, but I won't hurt you. I'll try my best to go slow and easy." He hoped he wouldn't prove himself a liar. He ached with need. Only release within her caressing body could ease his pain.

Reaching down, he grabbed his jeans up off the dark blue rug and rummaged in the pocket for the small packet that would offer them protection.

"I...I want you, but I'm afraid. I don't know much about...well, about being intimate with a man."

He lowered his big, hairy body down beside her. With the utmost care, he eased her clinging satin gown down her hips and legs. "There's no right or wrong way. Just act on your feelings and everything will be fine."

"That shouldn't be any problem because I feel so much for you," she whispered against his mouth as he pulled her into his embrace, tenderly brushing her lips with his.

He wished he had the strength to simply hold her until all her uncertainties vanished, but his desire for her was quickly eroding his good intentions.

Raising himself on one elbow, he looked down at her flushed face. With a shaky hand, he skimmed her body from her throat to the dark mound hidden beneath a pair of sheer midnight-blue bikini panties. Slipping two fingers under the elastic edge around her leg, he found the moist heat surrounding the heart of her womanhood. When she cried out, he swallowed the sound as he took her mouth in a thorough kiss. Damn, but she was hot. Hot and wet and wanting!

He increased the pressure of his mouth, loving her with bruising forcefulness. He moved his hands in frenzied passion up and down her body, from ribs to hips, from breasts to knees, longing to subdue her. He knew he had to take her soon or he'd die.

Leah struggled against his superior strength, twisting and turning, the thrusting movements of her body seeming to

THE WANDERER   127

inflame his desire. "Judd... please slow down. You're...
you're frightening me."

At first she thought he hadn't heard a word she'd said. He
continued exploring her body with his mouth, then slowly
stopped as he raised his head, his eyes searching hers.

Judd saw genuine fear in her big, blue eyes. Eyes that
were filled with tears. One moist droplet trickled down her
cheek.

"No, don't." He moaned, sliding his tongue across her
cheek, capturing her tears. "Don't cry."

"Please understand." She clung to him, despite her fear
and uncertainty. "I want you. I want you so much, but I'm
just not used to this. I'm as afraid of myself, of what I'm
feeling, as I am of you." She had never experienced anything like this—this raw, primitive need to mate.

"Don't be afraid of me, honey. I'm sorry if I was too
rough. It's just that I want you so much." He kissed her
damp forehead. He realized that she had no idea how he
felt, what torture he was experiencing, and there was no way
to explain without frightening her even more. "Slow and
easy. Just the way you want it. All right?"

"Yes, please." She relaxed, gazing up at him with total
trust and eager willingness. Her lips, swollen and red from
his loving, parted slowly on a sigh of surrender.

He stared at her, enjoying the sight of her from the beauty
of her face to the loveliness of her pale flesh, damp and
glowing in the muted light. His gaze lingered on her small,
perfect breasts. He brushed his fingertips across the sensitive points. "Tell me that you want me."

She shivered with throbbing pleasure at his touch, an ache
of intense longing surging deep inside her body. Her voice
locked in her throat, making an answer impossible. She lay
there gazing up at him, hoping he understood. He continued stroking her nipples for several minutes before easing his
fingers down to her waist and across her stomach to the top
elastic of her panties. Ever so slowly, he slipped his hand
inside the sheer blue silk, letting his fingers move unerr-

ingly toward the dark triangle between her legs. As he began to stroke her, she jerked convulsively, twisting her head from side to side. When he repeated the intimate caress again and again, she moaned into her fist.

Judd reached up, grasping her fist before leaning down to take one diamond-hard nipple into his mouth. Sucking gently at first, he gradually increased the pressure, eliciting a passionate cry from her.

Instinctively she reached for him, longing to draw him closer. When he covered her other breast with his mouth, arousing her to a fever pitch, she drowned in sensations her body had never known. All the while his mouth stimulated her breasts, his fingers worked their own magic. The power of his touch carried her over the brink into a shattering fulfillment. The ecstasy was so great, she wondered if she could survive.

"Was it good, honey? Did you like that?" Judd kissed the hollow of her throat, licking away the moisture from her flesh.

"Yes. I . . . oh, yes."

"There's more. So much more."

A raging hunger for some greater, unknown release filled her. She knew that only Judd's possession could take her beyond the pleasure he'd just given her.

"Judd," she said, her voice a raspy whisper of desire. "Please . . . please."

"Tell me what you want." He grasped her hands, holding them above her head.

"I want you."

"What do you want me to do?" Sweat dampened his face and curled the thick hair on his body. "And how much do you want it?" He longed to bury himself inside her hot, clinging body, to ease the ache that had tormented him for weeks on end.

"Make love to me." She rubbed against him. "I've never wanted anything so much."

THE WANDERER 129

Beginning a downward move, he explored her navel with his lips while he took hold of her panties, slowly gliding them down her hips and legs, freeing the hidden secrets of her body. With eager lips, he worshipped the discovery.

He lifted her hips, bringing her femininity up to his mouth. She clutched at his shoulders, groaning, squirming, pushing herself against his mouth, reveling in the agonized joy.

"Judd... oh, Judd!" Leah gave in to the wanton release.

The moment her body convulsed with a second climax, he moved his lips upward, across her stomach. He anointed her perspiring flesh with the moist, sweetness of his mouth.

"Don't be afraid to feel everything," he told her. "Give yourself to me completely. I want it all."

"Judd... I... I want you inside me." She arched upward, her body pleading. "No more slow and easy. Take me hard and fast. Take me now."

"Yes!" He answered her request, his mouth covering hers as his tongue rammed into the dark cavern of her mouth, her own tongue darting outward to slide against the harsh, driving pressure of his.

She wrapped her arms around his waist, urging him closer, enticing him to make the final move that would unite them in the ultimate joining.

Releasing her lips, he looked down at her. In a quick, sure move, he shielded himself. He nudged her legs apart and lifted her to him. With the utmost tenderness, he entered her, ever so slowly, easing more and more of himself into her. Then with one final thrust he claimed her.

"Leah...my Leah..." Her name, torn from his very soul, proclaimed his deepest emotions.

As the need for fulfillment increased, Leah moved rhythmically, encouraging Judd to give them both release. He quickened the pace of his plunges, delving again and again into the tight moist heat of her body. With one last thrust,

130   THE WANDERER

he propelled them both into an unbearably intense pleasure.

He eased his body from hers, keeping her close within the circle of his arms. Moving her head upward, she snuggled into the confines of his embrace, her dark hair falling across his naked shoulder. Breathing deeply, she began the progressive descent from the heights of sexual ecstasy to the dreamy bliss of satiation.

So this was what sex between a man and a woman was really all about, Leah thought. This unbelievable feeling of complete fulfillment. This wonderful contentment of loving and being loved.

Judd opened his eyes. Leah lay against him, her pale skin flushed and gleaming, moist and overly sensitive to his touch. She had wrapped her legs around his, the dark triangle of her feminine curls pressed against his hip and the bulging softness of her breasts pushing into his body, her nipples covered by his curling chest hair. He reached out, running his finger across her swollen lips.

She opened her mouth to speak, but he silenced her with a quick kiss. "Shh. Don't say it. Please don't say it."

She curled her fingers around his brownish-red chest hair, caressing him tenderly. "Not saying the words won't change the way I feel."

"What we feel is special," he admitted.

"It's never been like that with anyone else...ever." He felt her relax slightly. "Don't complicate things by putting labels on our feelings. We're good for each other. We're good together."

"For as long as it lasts?" she asked, wanting to confess her love for him, wanting his love in return, but knowing that he wasn't going to commit himself.

"You. Me. This..." He petted her intimately and smiled when she shivered. "As far as I'm concerned it could last forever. Just us and this incredible thing that happens between us."

THE WANDERER 131

She knew that in the bright light of day what he was offering wouldn't be enough. But now, tonight, in the sweet warm shadows of her private domain, she could accept only the wild hot needs of her body and forget all the rest.

"Stay the night," she said, moving closer, her body slipping atop his. Boldly she stared down at him. "Give me more. Make me—"

Reaching out, he pulled her mouth down to meet his while he grabbed her hips. When he pressed her against him, she moaned, feeling again the wildness clawing at her insides, demanding release. He slipped his hand between them, stroking her, encouraging her. Instinctively she rubbed herself against him. He hardened instantly.

His desire renewed so quickly that he had to force himself to stop, to think, to remember the risk involved if he didn't protect Leah—protect himself from the chance of an unwanted child. He took the proper precautions.

Raising herself up slightly, she looked down at their love-dampened bodies, her breasts grazing his chest. He shifted, lifting her hips over him and surging up inside her welcoming body. Moaning, she braced her hands above his shoulders, her fingers biting into his pillow.

"Come on, honey, ride me. Ride me rough and hard." He bucked upward, filling her completely.

The sound that came from her throat was a tortured mixture of sob and scream. With each consecutive thrust, she became more and more a willing participant, giving back as much as she was given. When he lifted her up and took one begging nipple into his mouth, she ground her hips into him. He ran his hands over her buttocks, soothing, absorbing the rhythm of their undulations.

Leah could feel the pressure mounting. Her body reached out for the pinnacle, already knowing the pleasure that awaited, but a part of her wanted to prolong her journey toward ecstasy. "Judd...it's so...so wonderful. You're so..."

132   THE WANDERER

His mouth moved from breast to breast, licking, sucking, nipping, increasing the frantic tension coiling tighter and tighter within her. The slightly abrasive scratch of his beard and mustache against her flesh sent shivers of sensual pleasure shooting through her. She moved faster and faster as the feeling grew stronger and stronger.

"You're so hot and tight. And so wet," Judd groaned against her breast. "You're almost there, honey. Just a little more." He quickened the speed and depth of his thrusts and intensified the assault on her breasts. He grunted out, in the most basic of words, what he wanted and what she needed.

It hit her then. A screaming, scorching white-hot blaze of pleasure. Her climax came like a tidal wave, consuming her, washing away everything that existed except the ferocity of her fulfillment.

The sounds of her release triggered his own as he rammed into her one final time, shuddering uncontrollably as his own passion claimed him.

"Nothing could really be this good," he mumbled as he reached down and pulled the covers up over them.

Judd opened his eyes to the softly filtered sunlight streaming through the windows, casting a golden radiance across the room and across the beautiful sleeping woman cuddled against him. Last night he'd paid little attention to this room, not noticing much more than the huge antique bed. He looked down at Leah, so appealing in her slumber. How was he ever going to be able to leave her? He'd been in Marshallton too long already, and all the while he'd known that she was the only reason he stayed.

He glanced around the room, noting the high white ceiling, the unmoving wooden fan and the pale blue walls, adorned by a delicate flowered border around the the top. Furniture filled every corner, creating a crowded effect, a closed-in, homey feeling. The furniture was old and oak and decorated with intricately carved moldings. In one corner

THE WANDERER 133

stood a dresser topped with a slab of marble, and a matching washstand had been placed by the bed.

Judd sat up, allowing the covers to drop to his waist. Leah stirred beside him. He wanted to take her in his arms, to kiss her awake, and then he wanted to make love to her again. Three times last night had sated him on a temporary basis, but he knew that he'd never get enough of Leah. Of her passion. Of her tender and loving heart.

Taking a deep breath, he inhaled the aromas of the bedroom, scents he would always associate with Leah. A basket of peach potpourri sat atop an old trunk situated at the foot of the bed. The bottle of Joy perfume he'd given her for her birthday, along with an assorted arrangement of empty powder and perfume containers, lined the dresser. Her gown lay across the back of a cane-bottom rocker.

Leah's room reflected her own unique personality. It projected warmth and gentleness. It bespoke the kind of elegance and grace that had long ago gone out of fashion. The room was as old-fashioned as the woman, but as welcoming as she. He felt at home here. In this room. In this bed. With Leah.

"Good morning." Opening her eyes and smiling, Leah clutched the sheet, blanket and wedding-ring quilt she used as a coverlet, then scooted up in the bed to sit beside Judd.

Placing his arm around her, he pulled her close. "It is a good morning, honey. The best morning I've had in years."

"I feel the same way." She gazed up at him, wondering if he realized how much she loved him.

He kissed her, a quick yet powerful expression of his feelings. "You can't imagine how long it's been since I've been this happy."

He laughed. "As a matter of fact, I'm not sure I've ever been this happy."

"I know exactly what you mean." She slipped her arm around his waist. "Please tell me that last night meant as much to you as it did to me." Despite her doubts, Leah

134   THE WANDERER

longed to hear him say he loved her, that they could make their relationship work.

"It meant as much to me." He frowned, knowing that she would be hurt by what he had to say. "Maybe too much."

"But Judd—"

He covered her lips with his index finger. "I don't want to lose you, honey." He hugged her, savoring the feel of her naked body against his. "Maybe I should have left weeks ago, but I couldn't bring myself to leave you. And now...now..."

"And now what?" she asked, praying for a miracle, for a change of heart.

"And now I want to stay with you and be a part of your life. But I can't offer you marriage. Not now, maybe not for a long time. You make me consider a commitment. I've been wondering if it isn't time to start thinking about the future and put the past behind me."

"Then stay here, Judd, and let me help you put your life in order. I know you don't want to hear me say the words, but...I love you and I want to make you happy." Tears of joy mingled with tears of sorrow. The doubts and uncertainties could do nothing to diminish the wealth of love and happiness within her heart.

"I'm not sure I believe in love anymore. I don't even know if I'm capable of love. But I do want to make you happy." He held her away from him, clasping her naked shoulders. "Can't you see that's what concerns me so? The one thing you want more than anything is a child, and I can't...I won't father another child."

"You might change your mind."

"No." Releasing her, he ran the tips of his fingers across her cheek, brushing away a falling teardrop. "I want you to know, to understand what it's been like for me knowing that I'm responsible for my son's death."

When he looked into her eyes he was afraid he would see suspicion, perhaps even condemnation, but all he saw was

THE WANDERER
135

love and concern. He took her face in his hand, cradling her chin with his thumb.

"Oh, Judd, tell me what happened."

Dropping his hand away, he got out of bed, turning his back on Leah. She sat watching while he reached down for his jeans and slipped them up over his long hairy legs. Judd Barnett was gloriously male. Big, muscular and rugged. Leah felt an instant tug of arousal, a tingling anticipation deep in her belly.

With his jeans zipped but unbuttoned, he sat on the side of the bed and tossed Leah her gown. "If we're going to get down to some serious talk, then you'd better put on something, because I can't think of anything except your body with you sitting there naked."

Quickly Leah pulled the pink flannel nightgown over her head. Scooting beside Judd, she reached out and took his hand. "Tell me about your son."

Smiling at her, he squeezed her hand. He looked down at the floor, noticing the pale pink-and-peach rose pattern woven into the deep blue wool rug. "His name was Steven. He was the only good thing that came out of my marriage to Carolyn."

"How old was Steven?"

"Six." Judd cleared his throat. "He was big and strong and healthy. He had Carolyn's blond hair and my brown eyes." Judd pulled his hand out of Leah's clasp. Dropping both of his hands between his legs, Judd bent over slightly, staring silently down at the floor as he willed himself not to cry.

"And you loved him very much." Leah didn't try to touch Judd. She simply sat beside him.

"More than anything. But... but I let Carolyn have custody when we got the divorce." He jumped up and slammed his fist into his open palm. "Dammit, I should have known she couldn't handle the responsibility. It was my fault. I knew what she was like, how immature and flighty, but I was too damned busy making mill...with my job. I loved Steven, but he came second to my work."

"What happened to Steven?"

"He drowned." Judd wanted to be honest with Leah. He longed to tell her everything. But he couldn't bring himself to tell her that he was a multimillionaire. She loved him, genuinely loved him, for himself. It was a gift worth treasuring, one he couldn't bear to lose. "Carolyn's home had a backyard pool. Steven loved to swim. God, he was like a little fish."

"Did you teach him how to swim?" Leah asked.

"Hell, no! I didn't have time. Carolyn hired a..." Judd started to say private swim instructor. "He had lessons at the rec center."

"Tell me what happened." Leah wondered what sort of job had meant so much to Judd, what sort of profession had paid for a backyard pool.

He remembered the details of that day—the day he'd never forget no matter how much he wished he could. Carolyn had given Steven's nanny the day off, knowing that he was supposed to pick Steven up for a trip to the zoo that afternoon. How could he explain to Leah that his son had had a nanny? "Carolyn and Steven had spent the morning around the pool. I was supposed to pick him up for the afternoon, so when Carolyn got one of her migraines, she took some medication and lay down. She'd already ordered pizza for their lunch and told Steven to pay the delivery man, eat, and then change into dry clothes before I got there."

"Such a little boy to be given so much responsibility." Leah knew that if she ever had a child, she would be one of those petting, pampering, overprotective mothers who spoiled their children with love and attention. Poor little Steven. If only he'd been her child—hers and Judd's.

"At six he was already taking care of his mother." Judd laughed, the sound a tortured grunt. "I got held up with a client. It was the weekend...on a Saturday, and I couldn't

THE WANDERER 137

leave my job long enough to pick up my son on time." Judd choked back the tears that burned his throat, that clotted in his chest and constricted his breathing.

More than anything Leah wanted to reach out and touch him, to soothe the pain that had tautened his big body. She looked at his hunched back, strained with tension. "You ran late picking up Steven that Saturday..."

"He'd eaten the pizza, changed his clothes and watched television. Carolyn's medication had put her to sleep." Judd jumped up off the bed and began pacing the room. "If only I'd gotten there on time, Steven would still be alive."

Leah sat on the bed, watching the man she loved torture himself with the memories of something he could never change. She longed to help him, to ease his pain.

Judd rubbed his hairy face with both hands, then ran his fingers through his shaggy hair. "Steven gave up on me, so he changed back into his swim trunks and played around in the pool. We...we'll never know for sure exactly what happened." Tears filled Judd's eyes, dampening his long, auburn lashes. "I was nearly four hours late. I found Carolyn asleep on the couch in the den. The patio doors were wide open. I walked outside. I called for Steven. He didn't answer." Judd's voice was hoarse with emotion.

"You found him." Oh, dear Lord, he'd found his son drowned in the pool. And he'd blamed himself for being late. For putting business first. For giving his irresponsible ex-wife custody of their child.

"I found him. Floating in the pool." Tears streamed down Judd's face. He turned to Leah. She held out her arms. He went to her, dropping to his knees and placing his head in her lap. She stroked his head with gentle love, threading the long strands of his hair through her fingers.

"Oh, Judd. My poor sweet darling."

He gazed up at her, his face wet with tears. "It was all my fault. Don't you see? I killed him. I killed him!" Judd grabbed her around the waist and clung to her, burying his face in the warm comfort of her bosom.

138   THE WANDERER

She stroked and petted him, comforting as a mother would a child. "No, Judd, you didn't kill him. Don't you know that what happened to Steven was an accident? You weren't to blame and neither was Carolyn."

Judd's big body shook as Leah held him while he sobbed. She listened to his self-derisive mumblings, comforted him when he screamed out his anger and pain, and loved him all the more for being man enough to share his sorrow with her.

And later, when he was spent, his emotions drained, she lay with him in her great-grandmother's bed, holding him in her arms while he slept. Leah had never dreamed she could love someone so much. Finally, at long last, she understood what Aunt Myrt meant when she talked about grand passion.

Leah pulled her station wagon into the alley behind Country Class, got out and rushed toward Judd who stood in the open doorway. She flung herself into his arms.

Less than five hours ago, they'd shared a long, sweet interlude after he'd awakened, then he'd gone back to his room above the shop. They'd made plans to share dinner, and to discuss the future. But ten minutes ago, Judd had phoned her and told her he had to leave town immediately.

"Honey, I could have come back to your house." Judd held her tightly, praying that she would understand what he had to do. "I'm picking up a rental car over at Southland Inn. Taylor's made all the arrangements."

"What happened?" Leah asked, holding on to Judd tightly as he grabbed her shoulders and tried to put some distance between them. "You said that your brother called and there was a family emergency."

Judd realized that she was fighting him, trying to hold on to him out of fear. Dear God, didn't she realize that he didn't want to lose her, either? "The man you met at The Country Pub the night before your birthday...well...he wasn't an old friend. He was my brother."

THE WANDERER

Leah looked up at Judd. "Your brother? Jared is your brother?"

"Yes. I...I keep in touch with him. I gave him the number here at Country Class."

"Is something wrong with Jared? Is he sick? Has he had an accident?"

Judd forcefully pushed Leah out of his arms, but kept a tight hold on her shoulders. "Jared's fine. It's Carolyn."

"Your ex-wife?"

"She tried to commit suicide today."

"Oh, dear Lord!"

"Listen to me, Leah. I don't want to leave. Not now when you and I have so many things we need to work out, but..." Dropping his hands from her shoulders, he ran his fingers through his hair as he turned from her. "Dammit! Jared said that all the guilt that Carolyn has felt over Steven's death has finally come to a head. For years she suppressed it. But lately...lately she's been depressed and despondent. Not herself. Jared's tried to be there for her. Hell, he's always had a crush on Carolyn. He thought he was in love with her years ago and now she's using his feelings to... He doesn't love her and she doesn't love him, but that won't stop her from ruining his life. Don't you understand?"

"No," Leah admitted. "I'm not sure that I understand anything."

Judd whirled around, his eyes riveted to Leah. "I've got to be there for Carolyn... to see her through this. Otherwise, she'll cling to Jared. She'll manipulate him for her own purposes."

"What about you?" Leah asked. "Don't you think she'll manipulate you?"

"I'm immune to Carolyn's charm. I know her too well. She and I are both takers. We used, then discarded each other, and our son paid the price for our selfishness. But Jared's not me. Jared's a giver, not a taker."

"So you're going home to protect your brother, is that it?"

140   THE WANDERER

"That's a big part of it." Judd hesitated momentarily, wondering if Leah could understand he owed it not only to Jared but Carolyn. And, yes, to Bess. "It's a complicated story, honey, a long, complicated story."

"You think you owe it to Carolyn because she was your son's mother? Is that it?"

"Partly, yeah. I understand the guilt that drove Carolyn to try suicide. I've been doing the same thing for years now. I just chose a slower form of death." Judd reached out, brought Leah's trembling hand to his lips and brushed a soft kiss across her knuckles. "Carolyn's younger sister Bess has loved Jared since she was just a teenager. But he could never see Bess for the woman she was because he was so infatuated with Carolyn. Bess moved off and stayed away for years. Now she's back. I don't want to see those two lose their second chance at happiness because of Carolyn."

Leah brought Judd's hand to her cheek, rubbing it against her face. "For a man who's been running away from responsibility, you sound pretty committed to helping your family. I understand that kind of loyalty. I gave up everything I'd dreamed of having to take care of Larry and Lisa and Aunt Myrt. How can I fault you for standing by your family when they need you?"

Judd pulled her into his arms. "You're something, do you know that? I've got to be the luckiest guy in the world. Of all the men out there... and you fell in love with me."

Before Leah could respond, Judd smothered her face with kisses, then took her mouth hard and fast, consuming her with his love and gratitude. She accepted him, loving him completely, knowing that she would never love another man the way she loved Judd.

She prayed that once he went back to his old life he would be able to come to terms with his past and return to her ready for the future. In this one moment of pure, sweet love, Leah knew that she wanted Judd Barnett more than anything else. Even if he would never give her a child.

Eight

Leah stared at the solitaire diamond sparkling in the muted restaurant light. Holding the open box in the palm of his hand, Stanley Woolton gazed longingly at Leah, his black eyes filled with warmth and caring.

"You know how deeply I care for you," he said, removing the ring from its velvet cradle. He dropped the jeweler's box back in his coat pocket, then reached out for Leah's hand. "I want you to be my wife."

She couldn't believe that, after nearly a year of dating Stanley, after endless months of hoping he would ask her to marry him, he was finally proposing. But he was too late. He had waited until after she'd met Judd Barnett, until after she'd made love with Judd and learned what it meant to have a grand passion—until after she'd gone and gotten herself pregnant. She hadn't seen a doctor yet, but she was sure. She'd missed her period, something she never did, and the home pregnancy test she'd taken had been positive. Despite Judd's precautions, he had fathered a child—a child he didn't want. When Stanley began slipping the ring on her finger, Leah pulled away, jerking her hand from his gentle grasp. "I...I'm flattered, Stanley. Really, I am, but... but..."

"You need time to think about it?" Stanley's smile faded, but the warm look in his eyes remained. "I've tried not to rush you. And I think I've been a perfect gentleman the entire time we've been dating." He pulled the box from his pocket, hastily placing the ring inside.

"Oh, you have, Stanley. You have."

"I was even understanding when you seemed infatuated with that..." Lowering his voice, Stanley shifted his gaze quickly from left to right, scanning the nearby diners. "That worthless bum you had working for you for nearly three months."

"His name is Judd Barnett," Leah said. "And he was not a worthless bum. He was a man who'd had a terrible personal misfortune. He was trying to escape from the pain in his past."

"Be that as it may, he's gone now, and the whole town is better off without him." Nervously Stanley took hold of his conservative navy-and-gold striped tie, readjusting the knot. "You are aware of the fact that there hasn't been another robbery since he left town?"

"I don't want to hear this." Leah dropped her napkin on top of the table and stood, her hip accidently hitting the side of her chair.

Stanley stood, stepping quickly around the table and grabbing Leah by the wrist. "Please don't leave. Sit down. Sit down." He eyed the nearby customers who were glancing his way. "I promise not to say another word about Barnett. I brought you here for lunch today to propose. I wanted to make you happy, not upset you."

When Stanley tugged on her arm and gazed pleadingly into her eyes, she nodded and allowed him to seat her. She knew she was a fool to defend Judd. To Stanley or to anyone else. Judd had left town over a month ago, and except

THE WANDERER

for a phone call the first week, she hadn't heard from him since. In that brief phone conversation neither of them had even mentioned the night they'd spent together or what, if anything, it had meant to them. He'd told her that the doctors felt that his ex-wife was still suicidal and that only his presence was keeping her alive. Carolyn Barnett saw Judd as her strength. Leah understood, or least she tried to understand. Under other circumstances, she would have encouraged Judd's care and concern for another human being, but Leah loved Judd and she was carrying his child. She didn't want him spending endless days and nights with another woman, a woman to whom he'd once been married.

"You and I are ideally suited." After sitting down, Stanley leaned slightly across the table and reached for Leah's hand. She dropped both of her hands in her lap, then faced her luncheon companion. "We both were born and raised here in Marshallton," he said. "We have similar family backgrounds."

"I don't think you have anyone in your family quite like Aunt Myrt." Leah sat ramrod straight, wishing she had the nerve to be unmannerly and simply get up and leave.

"Well, no, of course not. I don't think anyone has a relative like her." Picking up his full glass of water, Stanley drank half the liquid, then set aside the glass. "We really need to discuss what you're going to do with your aunt once we're married."

"What do you mean? Why would I do anything with Aunt Myrt?"

"Well, everyone knows the woman should have been committed years ago, and if it hadn't been for your kind and overindulgent heart—"

"As long as I'm alive, Aunt Myrt will never be put in an institution!" Leah jumped up.

"Whatever's the matter with you?" Stanley asked, swallowing several times. "You're acting most peculiar. Not yourself at all. Is it...is it—" he lowered his voice to a whisper"—that time of the month?"

144 THE WANDERER

"No, it isn't," Leah said, glaring at Stanley, wondering how she could ever have considered spending the rest of her life with him.

"Then what's wrong? You keep taking offense at every little thing I say, and your actions are embarrassing me."

"Stanley, I...I can't agree to marry you. You see, I don't—"

"Say no more, my dear." He held up both hands in a stop signal. "I understand that you need a little time to think things over. I was married once, and I do know that you females have your own womanly ways and all. I'll call you tomorrow."

"Stanley..." When Leah saw that glazed we'll-work-this-out look in his eyes, she realized that now was not the time to give the man a piece of her mind. There would be time enough for that later, in a more private place. Although she had no intention of ever dating Stanley again, let alone marrying him, she didn't want to cause him any undue embarrassment. After all, it really wasn't his fault that he was such a...a...a weasel!

"Just consider what a nice future we could share."

"Fine," she said. "I'll think about our nice future."

"I'll be calling."

"You do that." Leah made a beeline for the exit, jerking her raincoat and umbrella off the wooden rack by the door. Hurriedly she opened the umbrella and rushed toward her station wagon. She felt confused and angry. With Stanley. With herself. But mostly with Judd. She needed a loving shoulder to cry on. She needed Judd, but since he wasn't available, she'd go to the one person who'd always been there for her, the one person whose illogical advice often made good sense.

"Good grief, sweetie, you need to get out of those wet shoes immediately." Myrtle Mae glared down at Leah's soaked navy heels, then grabbed her niece's dripping wet

THE WANDERER 145

umbrella from her chilled fingers. "Where's your raincoat?"

Stepping out of her one-inch pumps, Leah reached down, picked them up and headed for the kitchen. "I need to talk to you, Aunt Myrt. Come on in here and sit with me while I make us some hot tea."

Myrt followed Leah into the kitchen, the smell of cinnamon surrounding them the moment they entered. "I was just warming myself some of your apple pie when I heard you drive up," Myrt said. "And there's already hot water in the kettle."

After placing her shoes near the back door, Leah prepared two cups of steaming Earl Grey tea while Myrt sliced another piece of cinnamon-laced apple pie and slipped it into the microwave to warm.

"I wasn't expecting you home this time of day," Myrt said, laying down two blue checkered napkins on the table. "Why didn't you go back to the shop after your lunch with Stanley?"

Leah put the two cups of tea beside the napkins, then sat down, raising the warm liquid to her mouth and sipping. She glanced over at Myrt, who was removing the pie from the microwave. "Stanley proposed."

Myrt jerked around, her bright green eyes open wide and her purple-tinted lips rounded. "Marriage? Stanley Woolton proposed marriage?"

"Yes. He even had an engagement ring, and . . . and he tried to put it on my finger."

"Well, it was bound to happen sooner or later, but now that you've rejected him, then it's all over. Nothing to worry about, sweetie. Absolutely nothing. Stanley will find another woman in time." Setting the dessert plates on the table, Myrt pulled out a chair and joined Leah.

"I...I didn't exactly reject him." Leah picked up her fork and cut into the pie.

"You can't mean to say that you accepted his proposal!"

146   THE WANDERER

"No, I didn't accept. I...I just didn't make it clear to him that I was refusing."

"But you do intend to refuse him?"

"Yes, of course. I'll have to...now."

"Now that you've found your grand passion with Judd." Myrt sighed as she picked up her tea cup, her little finger curling in a genteel manner.

"Now that I'm probably pregnant," Leah said, looking squarely at Myrt.

"Pregnant? Oh, my, my. Pregnant. Does Judd know? Of course he doesn't or he'd be here instead of off God only knows where playing nursemaid to his ex-wife."

"Maybe I should tell Stanley that I'm pregnant and see if he still wants to marry me." Leah slumped in her chair, bracing her elbows on the table as she clutched her teacup.

"Don't be ridiculous. You and Judd will get married," Myrt said, then put a huge bite of pie in her mouth.

"I don't think that solution is a possibility. Judd doesn't want to get married and he definitely doesn't want a child."

"He'll change his mind when you tell him." Chopping off another bite of pie, Myrt wagged her fork at Leah. "Men have the oddest notions sometimes. It's up to us women to make them see reason. Just take Taylor, for instance. He insists that we can't get married until he saves up enough money to take me to Hawaii for a honeymoon. That could take years."

"Has Taylor heard from Judd recently?" Leah asked.

"You're the only one who's heard from him," Myrt said.

"Over three weeks ago and not a word since. I can't help but wonder if he'll ever come back to Marshallton."

"He'll be back. Mark my word." Myrt popped the last piece of pie into her mouth and smiled.

"I wish he'd never come into my life." Leah pushed aside her pie plate and teacup. Crossing her arms, she laid her head, facedown, on the tabletop. "Everything would have been fine," she mumbled. "I'd have married Stanley and...

THE WANDERER

and had his baby and...and never have known what it was like to have a grand passion. I'd have been so much better off."

Shoving back her chair, Myrt stood and walked around the table. Putting her arms around Leah, she reached out to turn her niece's tearstained face toward her. "You've been given a rare gift and you mustn't wish it away."

Leah could feel the tears lodged in her throat, the tears that threatened to choke her. "What am I going to do, Aunt Myrt? I'm thirty-nine and unmarried. And I'm pregnant. People are going to...to think that...that..."

"People are going to think that you and Judd Barnett were lovers and that you're going to have his baby." Myrt hugged Leah, then began rubbing her back soothingly. "I'd give anything if I were young enough to give Taylor a child."

Leah wiped the tears from her cheeks. She turned, staring at her aunt. "I shouldn't care what people think, should I?"

"I never have." Pulling up a nearby chair, Myrt sat beside her niece. "Why don't you go upstairs and take a nice hot bath? I'm expecting Taylor shortly. We're going to Memphis for the weekend, and we want to make our plans today."

"Taylor has made you very happy, hasn't he?" Leah placed her hand over her aunt's where it lay on the table.

"I know that Taylor is his last name, but for the life of me, I can't call him Bernard." Myrt giggled, her appleround cheeks crinkling with tiny laugh lines. "Besides his wife called him Bernie. Isn't that just awful?"

Leah and Myrt both laughed. "I was so afraid that he was taking advantage of you...when we first met him and...Judd."

"Poor man had lost everything and didn't have a soul he could turn to. After his Sarah's years in that nursing home suffering with Alzheimer's, Taylor had to sell his drycleaning business and his home to pay off all their debts." Myrt's eyes filled with tears. "He'd do the same for me, you

148 THE WANDERER

know. When a man like Taylor loves a woman, he'd do anything for her." She smiled.

"And he loves you very much." Leah flung her arms around her aunt, burying her face in Myrt's fleshy shoulder. "I envy you that love."

"And I envy you that baby growing inside you," Myrt said.

The back door swung open. A gush of damp, cold air swept into the room. Taylor set his umbrella in the corner, then looked at the two women who were staring at him, their eyes red and watery.

"What's going on here? Did somebody die?" Taylor asked.

Myrt got up and went over to Taylor. "Just silly girl talk. Too mushy for men."

"I thought you'd be down at the shop," Taylor said.

"She's feeling a bit under the weather." Myrt slipped her arm around Taylor's waist. "I've been trying to talk her into going upstairs and taking a nice hot bath."

"Well, she might want to wait on that a bit." Taylor squeezed Myrt's ample hip. "There's a fellow down at Country Class looking for her."

"Who?" Myrt and Leah asked simultaneously.

"Judd's back," Taylor said. "He came by the motel to see me. Said he was on his way down to Country Class to talk to Leah."

Leah jumped up, hurried across the room to find her shoes and hastily slipped her feet into them. "Is he all right? Is he going to stay now that he's back? Did he say what he wanted to talk to me about?"

"Calm down, Leah girl." Taylor reached out, placing his hands on her shoulders. "Call Pattie and tell her to have Judd come on over here."

"No. No. Aunt Myrt, call and tell her to have him wait for me there." Leah turned, rushing out of the kitchen. Myrt and Taylor followed her into the living room.

THE WANDERER 149

"You drive carefully. You hear me?" Myrt said, handing Leah her wet umbrella.

"I will. I will." Leah flung open the front door.

"And you tell him about the you-know-what." Myrt stepped out on the front porch to shout her last instructions.

Leah made a mad dash to her station wagon. Judd was back. Judd was back! Maybe, just maybe, everything was going to be all right.

She parked in the alley, made a mad dash to the back door and found it locked. Thunder boomed, shaking the windows. Leah tucked her purse under her arm, readjusted her umbrella and inserted the key. Just as the door swung open, her umbrella slipped to the ground. Hard rivulets of rain fell from the roof, drenching Leah's hair and face. Leaving the umbrella lying where it fell, she rushed inside, pulling the door closed behind her.

Judd wasn't in the storeroom. She wiped the moisture from her face and squeezed the water from her hair. She could hear voices—Pattie's and Judd's. Leah looked down at her clothes. Damp spots covered her navy suit. Her white cotton and lace blouse stuck to her chest.

Judd hadn't seen her in over a month, and dammit all, she probably looked like a drowned rat. But what did it matter how she looked? If Judd had come home to her, nothing else mattered.

"Leah?" Pattie called out from behind the checkout counter. "Is that you?"

Taking a deep breath and plastering a smile on her damp face, Leah marched out into the shop. Judd leaned against the counter, his big body slumped over slightly. Turning his head, he stared at her.

"Leah." Straightening, he took a tentative step toward her.

He'd changed so drastically that she barely recognized him. He still wore jeans and his tattered leather jacket, but his shirt was new and an expensive gold watch circled his wrist. But the most noticeable change was his short hair and clean-shaved face.

He saw the way she stared at him, as if he were a stranger. He rubbed his hand across his jaw and grinned. "Well, what do you think? Do I look a little more respectable?"

"You look . . ." She wanted to say that he looked wonderful. She wanted to run and throw herself into his arms. "You look fine."

"Quite a change, huh?" Pattie said. "At first I thought he was a customer. Until he spoke to me."

"I thought you'd be at work or I would have come by the house first," Judd said.

"I had lunch with Stanley and went home afterward to talk to Aunt Myrt." Leah shifted her feet, then glanced down at her soggy wet shoes. The rain had soaked through her clothes, chilling her body.

"What were you doing having lunch with Woolton?" Judd's voice held a sharp edge. The smile on his face faded quickly.

"Hey, look," Pattie said, coming out from behind the counter. "With the weather this bad, I doubt we'll have any more customers today. Why don't I just go ahead and close up shop? I've got a hot date with Fred tonight and I could use a little extra time to get ready."

"All right," Leah said. "You take care of everything out here." She glanced at Judd. Warm color stained his cheeks and menacing darkness stormed in his eyes. "Why don't we go in my office and talk."

Judd reached out, grabbing her by the arm. "Why don't we go upstairs to my old room? I left my suitcase up there, but, who knows, I might need to take a room at Southland Inn tonight."

Leah jerked away from him. "Are you upset because I had lunch with Stanley?"

He grabbed her arm again and practically dragged her into the back storeroom. He slammed the door. "Hell, yes,

THE WANDERER

151

I'm upset because you had lunch with Stanley. You have no right to be seeing him.''

"What do you mean by that?"

"How many times have you seen him since I've been gone?" Judd grabbed her by the shoulders.

"If it's any of your business, I have not been dating Stanley. I . . . I've had lunch with him a few times."

"How few?"

"Three times." She tried to pull away, but he held her firmly.

"You're not ever going to see him again. Do you understand?"

"No, I don't understand," she shouted, and tried again to free herself. The moment he loosened his hold, she pulled away. "I don't understand what's wrong with you. You've been gone for over a month. You called one time. One damn time!"

"Leah, listen to me. I—"

"No, you listen to me." Taking several steps toward him, she pointed her finger in his face. "I've been waiting and waiting and waiting for you to come back to me. When you didn't call, I made all kinds of excuses for you. But I've been afraid . . . so afraid that you'd never come back."

"Honey, I'm sorry. But that's no excuse to start seeing Woolton again. You should have known I'd come back as soon as I could." When he reached for her, she sidestepped his grasp.

"Stanley asked me to marry him," Leah said, her back to Judd.

"He *what?*"

"He wants to marry me. He's even bought a ring."

Judd thought about the diamond-and-sapphire ring upstairs in his suitcase. He'd chosen the ring because the blue stones reminded him of Leah's dark blue eyes. The ring wasn't the biggest diamond he could have bought, but he'd thought Leah would prefer something more delicate, a bit

152   THE WANDERER

more dainty and old-fashioned. "You're not going to marry Stanley Woolton."

She knew she wasn't going to marry Stanley, but she certainly didn't like Judd being so sure of her. After all, despite the fact that he'd finally come back to Marshallton, he'd been gone a long time. Judd Barnett had a lot of explaining to do. "I didn't give him my answer today."

"Then you can call him later and tell him no," Judd said as he reached out and took Leah's hand.

She didn't try to pull away because he held her so tenderly. She glanced at him, trying not to let her emotions overrule her common sense. All Judd had to do was touch her and she was putty in his hands. It wasn't fair that he held such power over her. "I need the answers to some questions first."

"Let's go upstairs," Judd said, lifting her hand to his lips. "It's been a long month, honey, and I've missed you."

Leah quivered from the top of her head to the tips of her toes. "We'll go upstairs, but we're going to talk. I want those answers." She jerked her hand away.

Judd followed her up the stairs that led to the empty storeroom he had turned into a makeshift apartment. A mattress lay in the corner. A straight-back wooden chair, an old card table and a portable radio were the only other items in the room except for his suitcase.

Leah whirled around, planted her hands on her hips and stared him directly in the eye. "Why were you gone so long? And why didn't you call more than once?"

"Leah..." When he walked toward her, she backed away and held up her hands in a warning signal. "Carolyn refused psychiatric help. We took her home and kept a close watch on her."

"We? Who's we?"

"Jared and I, and Carolyn's sister Bess... and a private nurse."

Leah walked around the room, nervously running her hand along the windowsill, dusting off the card table,

THE WANDERER 153

straightening Judd's suitcase where it lay across the chair. "How is Carolyn?"

"We're hoping she'll be all right." Judd wanted to take Leah in his arms, to make her understand that being away from her had made him realize how much she meant to him. He wanted to work things out with her, to spend the rest of his life making her happy. "Carolyn tried to kill herself again. She tried to drown herself in the pool. Jared saved her."

"Oh, Judd, how horrible for you...for all of you." Leah forced herself not to rush to him, take him in her arms and comfort him. She had to keep her distance, or she'd be lost. She ran her hands across the top of the radio, then began fiddling with the dials.

"It was the most difficult for Bess, seeing how concerned Jared was for Carolyn. She's still in love with my brother. I'm sure of that. And after Jared rescued Carolyn from the pool, he became her shadow."

Leah flipped on the radio. An old Righteous Brothers melody filled the room. "Soul and Inspiration." Judd came up behind her, covering her trembling hand with his own. "I stayed because I was needed. Carolyn needed me, but more importantly my brother needed me. He still does...but, I had to get back here to you. I couldn't stay away any longer."

"Why...why didn't you call?" Leah turned. He was so close their bodies almost touched.

He squeezed her hand. "When I left here, I was very confused about my feelings for you. I knew that I wanted you more than I'd ever wanted a woman. I couldn't bear the thought of losing you, but I was aware of how much you wanted a child..." He noticed her face turn pale as tears gathered in the corners of her eyes. "Leah?"

"You haven't finished answering my question." Dear Lord, how was she ever going to be able to tell him that she was pregnant?

154   THE WANDERER

"I knew that I could never give you the thing you wanted most. I decided that it would be better for both of us if I could forget you, if I didn't come back to Marshallton."

Tears escaped from her eyes and trickled down her cheeks. "You didn't call because... because you weren't going to come back?"

"Leah, I honestly thought it was the best thing I could do for you."

"Then why are you here? And why did you get so angry when I told you about Stanley's proposal?"

He pulled her to him. She went into his arms without protest. "While I was away, trying to be so noble, trying to help my family and stay away from you, I discovered one very important thing."

"What?" His lips were so close, so very, very close.

"I discovered that I don't want to live without you."

"Judd?"

"Dammit, Leah, tell me that you still love me. Tell me that you'll forgive me for being such an idiot." His lips hovered over hers as he pressed his body closer.

"I still love you," she whispered. "I love you more than ever." She thought of her child, Judd's child, and knew that somehow she'd have to find a way to tell him.

"Leah..." He took her mouth, tenderly at first, almost hesitantly.

Her eager response ignited a fire of passion within him. He deepened the kiss, invading her mouth with frenzied thrusts. She clung to him, her arms draped around his waist. Dropping his hands to her hips, he pulled her up against him.

"When A Man Loves A Woman" began playing on the radio. Both of them heard *their* song. They gazed into each other's eyes, the desire so strong it became a visible thing, glowing brightly like a raging forest fire.

"You're soaked to the skin," he said, running his hands up and down her arms. "Come on, honey, let's get you out of these wet clothes."

THE WANDERER

She stood in the middle of the partially empty storeroom, the only light coming through a small, high window. Gray shadows embraced her. Damp, cool air caressed her as Judd removed her jacket.

He unbuttoned her blouse with slow, trembling fingers. "I've missed you so." Leaning over, he kissed her throat.

Leah quivered. The touch of his lips was like fire. Tossing her hair back, she tilted her chin upward and gave herself over to Judd's care.

He slipped the blouse from her shoulders, letting it drop to the floor. Closing her eyes, she reveled in the feel of his big hands soothing over her moist skin. He unsnapped her bra, then eased it away from her body.

He pulled her wet skirt down her hips. "Damn panty hose," he said, inserting his fingers beneath the waistband. "I'd like to shoot the idiot who invented these things." He tugged the nylon material down and off.

Stepping out of her panty hose, Leah glanced at Judd. He stared at her, taking in every inch of her body. "I want to undress you," she said, then proceeded to remove his leather jacket.

"You'd better hurry, honey. I don't think I can wait much longer."

Leah's fingers shook when she tried to unbutton his shirt. "Maybe you'd better do it. I...I..."

Judd shed his shirt, jeans and briefs, then kicked off his shoes and ripped off his socks. When he stood up straight, he smiled at her. "Come here, honey."

She obeyed instantly, going into his open arms. He covered her buttocks with his hands, grasped her bikini panties and eased them down her legs.

He buried his face between her breasts, gripping her hips, bringing their naked bodies together. Leah cried out, clinging to his shoulders. Moving his mouth from one breast to the other, Judd lavished attention on each pouting nipple.

156 THE WANDERER

Desire tugged unmercifully at her, a hot, wild sensation spiraling out from her lower body. "Judd...Judd...please, darling...please..."

Lowering himself to his knees, Judd kissed her belly, delving his tongue into her navel, then painting an uneven line downward. Leah went limp, her knees weakening. She swayed. Judd held her hips firmly as he nuzzled her.

"There hasn't been one day that I haven't thought of you," he said. "There hasn't been a minute that I didn't want to be with you."

"Please, don't ever leave me again." She threaded her fingers through his hair, moaning when his lips touched her intimately.

Judd stood, lifted Leah into his arms and carried her across the room. He lowered her onto the mattress, applied the protection he always used, and came down to her. Kissing her repeatedly, passionately, Judd entered her and together they groaned with pleasure.

"I can't wait," he said, surging into her, his thrust deep and hard.

"I don't want you to slow down...this time." She raised her hips, joining him, encouraging his wild frantic mating.

"We've got all night, honey. All night."

"Yes, we do." She sighed.

His big body overpowered her, taking her with such force that she struggled to keep pace with him. And when they both reached fulfillment, they slept briefly, then awoke aroused and wanting.

Evening turned to night and night into dawn—and the loving never stopped.

Nine

Leah put the finishing touches on her makeup, then swept her long dark hair up into a neat bun at the back of her neck. Adjusting the collar on her powder-blue sweater, she turned and faced Pattie.

"How can I ever thank you?" Leah gave her friend a hug. "It's embarrassing enough that you and Aunt Myrt and Taylor know I spent the night upstairs with Judd, but if I'd had to leave here this morning and drive home in my wrinkled clothes, someone would have seen me and spread the word all over town."

"Don't thank me," Pattie said, grinning. "Thank Aunt Myrt. She's the one who called and asked me to stop by and pick up a change of clothes for you."

"Are you decent?" Judd asked as he opened the storeroom door and peeped in.

"Well, we're both dressed," Pattie said. "Come on in. Did you get our sausage biscuits?"

158   THE WANDERER

Judd held up a white paper sack. "Right here. Did you make the coffee?"

Pattie pointed to the coffeemaker, the pot filled with piping-hot brew. "Hand over the grub. I'm starved."

Delving into the sack, Judd tossed Pattie a wrapped biscuit, then set the paper bag on the counter. He walked over to Leah, took her chin in his hand and pulled her face into his kiss.

"Ain't love grand?" Pattie poured herself a cup of coffee. "I can see you two want to be alone. I'll be out front tending to business."

When Judd ended the kiss, Leah glanced across the room just in time to see Pattie close the door behind her. "She's the best kind of friend."

Judd put his arm around Leah's shoulder, pulling her close. "You and I need to have that long talk we put off last night. I've got a lot to tell you, honey, and I hope you're going to understand why I haven't told you before now."

"My goodness, you sound so serious." Leah laughed, leaning her head against Judd. "You aren't a wanted criminal, are you?"

"No, but you might wish I were when I tell you what I really am."

"Don't you know that nothing you tell me is going to change the way I feel about you?"

"I'll hold you to that." He walked her over to a wooden stool, lifted her and set her atop the padded seat. "I hardly know where to start." Reaching down, he pulled her hands up from where they rested in her lap.

"I love you, Judd Barnett."

"And I—"

"Mac, don't you dare go back there!" Pattie yelled.

Shoving the door open, Lieutenant McMillian stormed into the storeroom. Pattie ran in behind him.

"He said he had to see Judd." Frantically Pattie waved her hands about in the air. "I told him that I'd come get you, but he wouldn't wait."

THE WANDERER 159

"What seems to be the problem, Mac?" Judd asked, releasing Leah as he turned to face the policeman.

"My problem is you, boy." Mac swaggered over, stopping directly in front of Judd. "You should have stayed gone."

Leah scooted down off the stool. "Mac, you have no right to harass Judd this way." She slipped her arm over Judd's.

"I'm afraid I do, Leah," Mac said. "I've come here to arrest your friend."

"What?" Pattie gasped.

"On what charges?" Leah asked.

"After Mr. Barnett left town, our downtown robberies stopped. But the first night he's back, Gibson's Hardware gets hit." Mac pulled out his handcuffs.

"That's a coincidence," Leah said, tightening her hold on Judd's arm. "You don't have any proof."

"We've got an eyewitness who saw Barnett coming out of the hardware store about midnight last night." Mac reached for Judd's hands.

Judd glared at Mac. "Who's your witness?"

Mac dropped his hand atop his holster. "Are you going to give me any trouble, boy?"

"Who's your witness?" Judd repeated his question.

"Trey Woolton," Mac said. "He was out carousing with some of his buddies when he saw you."

"He's lying." Leah walked in front of Judd, putting herself between the man she loved and the lawman. "There is no way Judd could have been seen coming out of Gibson's Hardware at midnight last night."

"And just why is that?" Mac asked.

"Because . . . well, because he was . . . was . . ."

Judd stepped around Leah, held his hands out in front of him and gave her a warning look. "Because she knows I'm not a thief. She trusts me. Don't you, Leah?"

"Yes, of course I do, but . . ." Leah couldn't believe this was happening. All she had to do to stop this ridiculous arrest was to tell Mac that she'd spent the night with Judd. But

160   THE WANDERER

Judd didn't seem to want her to give him an alibi. What was
he trying to do, protect her reputation?

"Put the cuffs on, Mac. I'll come peacefully." Judd accepted the handcuffing, listening patiently while Mac read
him his rights.

"Judd?" Leah followed them to the front door.

He stopped, then turned to face her. "It's all right, honey.
I'll get one phone call. Jared will have me a lawyer by the
time Mac gets me booked."

"Please, just let me—"

"No need," he said, bending over to kiss her on the
cheek. "It's about time this town found out just who they're
dealing with. I may have been a shiftless wanderer for the
past few years, and people like Mac here and Stanley and his
worthless kid may think they can railroad me, but they're
wrong."

Leah rushed out onto the sidewalk, following Judd as
Mac led him to the police car and shoved him inside. When
they drove off, she turned to Pattie, who took her into her
arms.

"I've got to get down to the police station. I don't know
why he wouldn't let me tell Mac the truth," Leah said.

"Oh, I think Judd was playing knight in shining armor,
trying to protect your reputation. He knows how important
appearances are to you." Pattie stroked Leah's back.

Leah stepped out of Pattie's arms, wiped the tears from
her eyes, and went inside Country Class. "I don't want my
reputation protected. I don't give a damn what anybody in
this town thinks. I love Judd Barnett." Leah marched back
out onto the sidewalk. "Do you here me, Marshallton,
Tennessee? I love Judd Barnett, and I spent the night with
him last night. All night. Right up there." She pointed toward the second floor of her shop. "And I'm going to have
his—"

Clamping her hand over Leah's mouth, Pattie dragged
her inside, slamming the door hard enough to make the glass
panes rattle. "Have you lost your mind?"

THE WANDERER 161

Leah jerked away from her friend. "So what if I have? Maybe insanity runs in the family. I'm probably more like Aunt Myrt than I ever imagined."

"Well, I know one thing," Pattie said. "Falling in love with Judd Barnett has certainly given you guts. Do you realize that you just came very close to telling the whole town that you're pregnant?"

"I did, didn't I?"

"Yes, you did. Don't you think you should tell the father first?"

"Oh, Pattie. I've got to get down to the police station and straighten out this whole mess."

"We'll lock up. I'm coming with you."

"Fine, but call Aunt Myrt and Taylor first. Judd's going to need all his friends."

Leah marched into Chief Rayburn's office, Pattie, Taylor and Aunt Myrt trooping in behind her like a three-man infantry charge.

"Judd Barnett did not rob Gibson's Hardware last night, despite what Trey Woolton might have told you," Leah said.

"Leah—" Hink Rayburn tried to respond, his big blue eyes widening as a pink flush darkened his Porky Pig cheeks.

"He was with me. All night." Leah hammered her fist down on top of the chief's desk. "Do you understand? We were upstairs in the storeroom above my shop from three-thirty yesterday until after Pattie came to work this morning."

"Leah, there's really no need for you to do this," Chief Rayburn said. "Everything's been—"

"I'm his alibi, dammit. Judd Barnett was making love to me at midnight last night, not out robbing the hardware store."

"You'd better listen to her, Hink." Myrtle Mae sauntered up to the chief's desk. "A woman in love is a powerful force to be reckoned with, you know."

162   THE WANDERER

"You can't fight all of us," Pattie said. "Trey Woolton is a spoiled, hateful brat and you know it. He's despised Judd ever since Judd came to town."

"Ladies, ladies...please calm yourselves." Hink Rayburn rose to his five-feet eight-inch height. "There wasn't any need for y'all to get your dander up this way and come flying in here like a pack of avenging angels. Mr. Barnett's lawyer has taken care of everything."

"His lawyer?" Leah asked.

"Peyton Rand," the chief said.

"How on earth can Judd afford Peyton Rand?" Pattie shook her head in disbelief.

"My brother arranged for Mr. Rand's services." Judd walked into the chief's office.

Turning, Leah smiled, relief spreading through her when she saw Judd. "They didn't book you?"

"It seems that Chief Rayburn has had his eye on a different suspect for quite some time, and when that suspect came forward as an eyewitness against me, the chief's suspicions escalated." Judd put his arm around Leah. "Trey Woolton and his buddies are in big trouble."

"What?" Leah stared at Judd, wondering if she'd heard him correctly.

"Doesn't surprise me a bit," Myrtle Mae said.

"Well, I'll be." Taylor slapped Judd on the back. "All this hullabaloo for nothing."

"Yep, we got a search warrant for the Woolton house while Mac was out arresting Mr. Barnett. Trey had no idea that he and his friends were under investigation. Anyway, we found some of the stolen goods in Trey's room and even more in the attic above the Woolton's garage."

A tall, robust man in his late thirties entered the room. He wore a custom-tailored business suit and carried a leather briefcase. His blond hair was cut short. His piercing blue eyes surveyed the occupants of the chief's office. "You're free to go, Mr. Barnett," Peyton Rand said. "Your brother is outside waiting for you in the limo."

THE WANDERER 163

"How'd he get here so fast?" Judd asked.

"Jared hired a helicopter and rented a limo." Peyton shook hands with his client. "You might want to leave soon. They've brought in young Woolton, and his grandmother is giving everybody out there holy hell."

"You just leave Cora Woolton to me." Myrtle Mae planted her hands on her wide hips. Tossing back her head, she paraded out into the station where the sound of Cora's screeching voice ended abruptly when she saw Myrtle Mae.

"Come on, Leah, let's leave this madhouse behind." Judd glanced over at Hink Rayburn. "Is there a back way out of here?"

"Go to the left, and down the hall. There's an exit onto fourth street."

"Thanks." Judd maneuvered Leah through the crowd of onlookers. "You and I have some major talking to do."

With her mind whirling from the unexpected turn of events, Leah followed Judd without question. When they saw Jared standing beside a long black limousine, Leah slowed her step.

"Judd, thank God!" Jared grabbed his brother's arm. "Peyton Rand said he'd taken care of everything. Are you all right?"

"I'm better than all right." Judd opened the limo door. "Go get some lunch or something. Leah and I are going to take a ride and make some decisions about our future."

Leah and Judd slipped into the back seat. After giving the chauffeur instructions to simply drive around, Judd turned to Leah, taking her into his arms. She snuggled close.

Sighing deeply, she gazed up at him. "Are you going to tell me what's—"

He kissed her on the tip of her nose. "We're getting married."

"We . . . we are?"

He pulled a jeweler's box from his pocket. Leah stared down at his hand. Flipping open the box, Judd removed an exquisite diamond-and-sapphire ring, then reached for

164   THE WANDERER

Leah's hand. She watched, speechless, while he slid the ring onto her finger.

"Judd, I don't understand anything that's happened today. I'm totally confused."

"You love me, and we're going to get married as soon as possible. What's confusing about that?" He kissed her ear, then nuzzled her neck.

"Do you love me?" He hadn't said the words, and she desperately needed to hear them. If he loved her, he might be able to accept the fact that she was carrying his child.

"Honey, love is just a word. I care for you in a way I've never cared for another woman. You've helped me more than you'll ever know. You've made me want to stop wandering and settle down. You've given me a reason to live."

She realized that Judd was still afraid to love, afraid of the risk involved. If he couldn't admit that he loved her, how would he ever be able to accept the fact that she was going to have his baby? Loving another child would pose an even greater risk, one she doubted Judd was willing to take.

"I want to say yes."

"Then say it and let's start making plans," he said.

Leah looked down at the ring on her finger. It was beautiful—and very expensive. "I want to be your wife. I want to spend the rest of my life with you, but... but I need to know what happened today and how on earth you can afford a lawyer like Peyton Rand, a ring like this... And what are we doing driving around town in a limousine?"

"Okay, honey, here goes." Judd kept his arms around her, not wanting to let go of her for a minute. "When Mac first started throwing accusations my way, I had Jared call in Peyton Rand, who had a talk with Chief Rayburn. The chief was already looking for other suspects. He isn't the idiot good ol' Mac is."

"Poor Stanley. And Cora! The scandal will devastate her."

"They raised that boy to think he was above the law just because of who his family is."

THE WANDERER 165

"Why would Trey and his friends steal? They didn't need the money."

"Who knows? For the thrill of it, or just to see if they could get away with it. Maybe, just out of meanness."

"Stanley didn't put him up to accusing you, did he?"

"No, honey, I don't think so. I figure that was Trey's own idea. He saw me, a poor drifter, as the perfect scapegoat. Unfortunately his plan backfired on him."

Leah leaned her head into the cushioned back seat, closed her eyes and sighed. "Judd, just how rich are you?"

He took a deep breath, praying that she wouldn't feel betrayed when he told her the truth. After all, she'd taken him in when she'd thought he was homeless. She'd given him a job, a place to live, and a loving heart filled with sympathy and concern. "I'm a multimillionaire. I'm chairman of Barnett, Incorporated. We own Southland Inns."

"Oh . . . my . . . God . . ."

"Honey, I left it all behind and started wandering aimlessly around the country after Steven died. I hated the company and I hated myself." Taking her face in his hands, he stared into her moist blue eyes. "I know I should have told you, but . . . for the first time in my life I knew what it felt like to have someone love me just for myself."

"Oh, Judd, I can't imagine a woman loving you for any other reason."

"Leah Marshall, you're the best thing that ever happened to me."

"There's one more thing I have to ask. It's something far more important than why you've kept secrets from me."

"I know that you're hurt—"

"Yes, I guess I am. I shared everything with you, told you all my heart's desires and secret pains."

"I promise that I'll never keep anything from you again. Total honesty from now on. For the rest of our lives."

"Judd, what about children? Will you let me give you a child?" She felt him stiffen, his whole body going rigid.

166   THE WANDERER

"Leah, I can give you anything that money can buy. I can make you happy, but...but I can't give you a child. I won't put myself through that pain again. I can't risk it. Not for anyone. Not even for you."

"I see." Tears filled her eyes.

"We can have a full and complete life without children. We'll have each other, and I'll never let anything or anyone ever hurt you." He spread tender, pleading kisses over her face, clutching her with desperation, so afraid she would reject him.

Leah wanted to marry Judd. She wanted to spend the rest of her life waking up in his arms. But what would happen when he found out that she was pregnant? He didn't want a child. Would he insist on an abortion? She couldn't take the chance. She knew she had to choose between Judd and their unborn baby.

"I can't marry you. I...I want children. I..." Giant sobs invaded her chest, restricting her breathing, choking her. She slipped the ring off her finger and handed it to him.

"Leah, don't do this. Don't throw away what we could have because you think you have to have a baby." Balling his hands into tight fists, he clutched them in front of him.

Prizing one of his fists open, she laid the ring in his palm. "I love you. Remember that...and if you ever change your mind, I'll be here." *Your child and I*, she said silently. *We'll wait for you forever.*

"Leah, please, honey."

"Ask the driver to stop. I'll walk home."

"How can you do this? If you loved me as much as you say you do, you'd come with me and be my wife, despite the fact that you want a child and I don't."

Leah knocked on the glass barrier that separated the chauffeur from the limo's occupants. "Stop the car, please. I want to get out."

"Stop now," Judd said. "The lady wants to leave me."

The moment the limousine came to a halt, Leah flung open the door and jumped onto the sidewalk. With her hand

THE WANDERER
167

on the handle, she looked at Judd, trying to memorize his face, knowing she might never see him again.

He leaned across the seat. "Leah..."

"Goodbye, Judd."

"If you change your mind, you can contact me at Barnett, Incorporated in Memphis." Dammit! He wanted to drag her back into the limo and take her away with him. Sooner or later she was bound to come to her senses about this baby business. He could give her so much. Why couldn't she be satisfied without demanding the one thing he couldn't give her?

"And if you change your mind—"

"I won't," he said.

"I love you. I'll love you always." Slamming the door, she walked away, hot salty tears blinding her. She stopped dead-still when she heard the limousine drive away.

Ten

Jared slammed the door, marched over to Judd's desk and picked up the telephone. He flung the receiver at his brother. "Call Taylor."

"What the hell's the matter with you?" Judd caught the receiver, then set it back onto its cradle atop his desk.

"I've had all I can take." Jared ran his fingers through his dark hair. "And it's not just me. It's everybody around you. You've lost four secretaries in the six months since you've been back at Barnett, Incorporated."

"Is it my fault that they were inept?"

"They were all perfectly good employees. You were at fault. Not them." Jared leaned over, flattening his hands out on Judd's desk. "You're miserable. You're eating your heart out over Leah Marshall, but you haven't got the guts to make a real commitment to her."

"We've discussed this before. As recently as last week, and nothing has changed since then. Leah knows how to get in touch with me if she wants me. Obviously she's been able

THE WANDERER 169

to live without me for six months.'' Judd knew that Leah hadn't married Stanley Woolton and she wasn't even dating anyone else. He talked to Taylor almost every week, and their conversations altered little each time they spoke. Leah was fine, but lonely and unhappy. Hell and damnation! If she was so unhappy without him, why didn't she come to him? She knew he wanted to marry her.

''I imagine she's waiting for you to come to your senses,'' Jared said, hammering his fist on the desk. ''She wants a baby, or have you conveniently forgotten that little detail.''

''I don't want—''

''You don't want, you don't want! Listen to yourself. After nearly four years of guilt and misery, you're still the same self-centered bastard you used to be.'' Jared pulled back, away from his brother, his gray eyes riveted to Judd's hard face. ''For once in your life think about somebody besides yourself.'' Jared walked away, closing the door quietly behind him.

Judd propped his elbows on his desk. Burying his face in his open palms, Judd rubbed his eyes and forehead. Sometimes the truth hurt, and he was sure Jared had meant for his words of truth to not only hurt, but to enlighten. Judd knew his brother loved him—loved him enough to be honest with him.

He was a selfish bastard. He always had been. He'd been taught by their father—a true expert. Luckily Jared was smarter. He'd seen their father for what he was long before Judd realized that he was mimicking the man whose actions he most despised.

Ten years ago Carolyn Cochran had wanted him, and he'd found her father's business and her sexy body an irresistible combination. He'd married Carolyn, not loving her. And not once caring whether she loved him. Out of their selfish, unhappy marriage had come a child. Pure and innocent. A child they'd both loved, but neither had taken the time to cherish and protect. When Steven had died, Judd, in his typically selfish way, had thought of no one but him-

170   THE WANDERER

self. The pain and guilt had almost destroyed him. Then he'd found a happiness he didn't think existed when he fell in love with Leah. But she had wanted more than he was willing to give. Selfishly he had not been able to put her wants and needs before his own.

In one brilliant flash of self-discovery, Judd realized that he was indeed just what his brother had called him. A selfish bastard. He didn't deserve Leah, and he certainly didn't deserve another child. But he wanted Leah. He wanted the chance to prove to her that he was capable of true love, the unselfish, giving kind of love that she needed. And, although he was afraid of loving another child and taking the chance of losing it, he wanted a child. Leah's child.

Picking up the phone, he dialed the number for Southland Inn in Marshallton. He smiled when he recognized Taylor's voice.

"Taylor, it's Judd. How are you?"

"Doing just great. You?"

"I've been better. Jared says I'm creating a real problem around here, eating my heart out for Leah."

"Well, she's got a better disposition than you do, so the only body she's making miserable is herself."

"Does she ever ask about me?" Judd had wondered if she thought about him all the time the way he did her.

"Every time you call, I tell her how you're doing."

"Does she . . . do you think she still cares?"

Taylor grunted. "Myrtle Mae says that you were Leah's grand passion. A woman never gets over her grand passion."

"What does Leah say?"

"Why don't you ask her?"

"I've been a fool, haven't I? I've wasted six months waiting for her to come to me on my terms, when all along I should have been down on my knees begging her to forgive me."

"It's not too late," Taylor said. "You've got about two months to make things right."

THE WANDERER   171

"What's happening in two months?" Dear God, had she met someone else? Had she finally agreed to marry Stanley Woolton?

"Why don't you come to Marshallton and find out?"

"All right, I'll come to Marshallton. You can expect me tomorrow." Just before Judd hung up the phone, he heard Taylor's hearty laughter and wondered what his old friend found so amusing.

The sleek, black limousine progressed rapidly in an easterly direction, Judd and Jared Barnett riding in silence. The limo traveled at top speed along a desolate stretch of highway miles outside of Memphis, slowly but surely moving closer and closer to Marshallton.

"What did Pattie say when you called her?" Judd asked.

"Not much. Just that she knows Leah still loves you, but that things have changed." Jared stretched out his long legs and readjusted his big body, leaning against the door.

"What could have changed?" Judd rubbed the back of his neck, hoping to ease the tight tension pains. "And why is she being so secretive? And Taylor. He's my old pal, but he acts like he has to protect Leah from me. Did Pattie give you any idea what's going on?"

"Yeah, she did," Jared said. "But I'm only guessing at what the problem is with Leah, so it's best if you just wait until you see her."

"If there is no other man and she still loves me, then what could be wrong? What's the big secret everyone is so concerned about?"

"If it's what I think it is, big brother, then you're going to get the chance to prove to Leah right away how much you love her." Jared leaned back against the seat, closing his eyes.

Judd knew that Jared had ended the conversation. Whatever Jared knew or thought he knew, he wasn't about to share. Judd glanced down at his watch. Thirty more minutes and they'd be in Marshallton. Thirty minutes and

172   THE WANDERER

his whole future would be decided by one dark-haired, blue-eyed woman who had no reason to give him another chance.

Judd leaned back, resting his head on the seat. He shut his eyes and pictured Leah. Beautiful Leah, gazing at him with wonder, her lips parted in a sigh of pleasure, her body loving and giving as he brought her to the very edge of rapture and watched as he carried her with him to fulfillment. Damn! How had he lived six months without her?

The humid September air combined with the sultry late-summer sunshine. Leah longed for autumn, for her favorite season of sweater weather. Summer sales were under way and business was booming. Even though Country Class usually did well this time of year, she realized that many of her customers were as interested in the shop's proprietress as they were the merchandise. And who could blame them? After all, she was a pregnant spinster who didn't seem the least embarrassed by her condition, which wasn't quite the norm for Marshallton, Tennessee.

Of course, Aunt Myrt was in her element defending Leah to all and sundry.

Leah had grown accustomed to the stares and whispers. She ignored any sympathetic questioning. She prayed that, by the time her child was born, the town would have become accustomed to the fact that Leah Marshall had dared to have a child without first acquiring a husband. Pattie had told her that, after the first few days of speculation about the identity of the father, ninety-nine percent of the locals were sure it was Judd Barnett.

Dear Lord, there was no way to keep a secret in a small town, especially a small Southern town.

"How many more boxes of Halloween stuff are there?" Pattie sat on the floor of the storeroom, her jean-clad legs crossed Indian style. "I could swear we've already unpacked a dozen."

THE WANDERER

"We've unpacked five very small boxes," Leah said. "There are three more to go. We'll need to put all of this on display soon. Halloween is only a little over a month away."

Pattie looked at her watch, then smiled up at Leah. "Where did the summer go?"

"If the weather is any indication, it's still here." Leah ripped open another small cardboard box. "Oh, guess what came in this morning?" Leah sounded like a delighted child who'd just received an unexpected gift.

"Besides all these crates and boxes?" Pattie spread her arms wide to point out the new merchandise.

"The cradle," Leah said. "The oak cradle. I haven't uncrated it yet, but I can't wait to see it."

"Why don't we open it now, and take it out to the shop and show Aunt Myrt?"

"We need to get these Halloween items checked first, but I'm a little worried about leaving Aunt Myrt out front by herself for too long. Maybe you should go check on her and make sure she doesn't sell the entire business at half price."

Standing and dusting her hands off on her jeans, Pattie laughed. "Aunt Myrt can't bear to see a customer leave the shop without buying something. That's why she keeps reducing prices until she talks them into a purchase."

"Were you girls speaking unkindly of me?" Myrtle Mae, decked out in a purple pants suit that matched her dark lavender lipstick and nail polish, entered the storeroom, her green eyes sparkling with amusement.

"Just wondering how long it would be safe to leave you on your own," Leah said.

"As you can see, I'm no longer tending to business. Taylor's here and he's playing cashier," Myrt said.

"Pattie, go on out front and give Taylor a hand." Leah sorted through the box she held. "Aunt Myrt, why don't you head home and put supper on the table? Everything's ready and in the refrigerator. Ham, potato salad, deviled eggs—"

174   THE WANDERER

"There'll be plenty of time for that later." Turning, Myrt followed Pattie out into the shop. Placing her hand on the younger woman's shoulder, she asked, "Do you want to tell me or do I have to interrogate Taylor?"

Pattie turned to Myrt, feigning puzzlement. "What are you talking about?"

"Don't mind her," Leah called out from the storeroom. "She's been acting strange all day. More so than usual."

"There's something going on," Myrt said. "Today's your regular off day, but you've been here all afternoon. And Taylor took off from work early. You've both invited yourselves over for supper, and told Leah to make sure there was plenty of food. So, I want to know what's going on."

"I don't have the faintest idea what you're talking about." Pattie shrugged.

"All right, if that's the way you want to be." Myrt walked quickly past Pattie, making a beeline for the cashier's desk where Taylor stood checking out an attractive young blonde with an infant on her hip.

"Behave yourself, Aunt Myrt," Leah said, walking over to the storeroom doorway. "Come back in here and help me. Leave Pattie and Taylor alone."

"I have no intention of being left out of this," Myrt said in a loud voice that gained her the immediate attention of several browsing customers.

"What are you talking about, love?" Taylor asked.

"Don't you *love* me." Myrt shook her finger in his face. "I know very well that you and Pattie have some sort of little fiasco going on here, and I want in on it." Myrt's short, round body trembled with agitation. "If you're trying to do something to help Leah, then I want to know what it is. I want to provide my assistance."

"Provide your..." Taylor glanced across the room at Pattie, who was shaking her head. "Go on home, Myrt, and get supper ready."

THE WANDERER

"I saw that." Myrt's face turned a darker shade of red than her bright hair. "I knew it. I knew it. You and Pattie are definitely up to something."

Leah tried to block out the sound of her aunt's scolding voice, but she couldn't erase her own suspicions. Both Pattie and Taylor had been acting strangely since yesterday. She couldn't imagine what, if anything, was going on, but she suspected a surprise baby shower might be their deep, dark secret, and both of them knew that Aunt Myrt could never keep a secret.

Leah closed the storeroom door. She knew that she needed to finish checking this new order, but what she really wanted to do was show Aunt Myrt and Taylor and Pattie the cradle that was still packed in its shipping container. All she had to do was close her eyes to picture herself rocking her little girl back and forth in the antique oak cradle.

Leah covered her stomach with her hand, caressing the bulge where her child nestled, safe and secure. Her child and Judd's. A child he would never know existed.

Judd Barnett came barreling through the front door, his brother following. Judd glared at the array of astonished customers who were staring at him.

"Well, well, well." Myrt grinned. "It's about time you showed up. If you'd waited another couple of months—"

"Good to see you. Yes, sir, mighty good to see you." Taylor dashed out from behind the counter, making his way hurriedly toward Myrt. He placed his arm around her, giving her a loving hug and a warning look. "Ever since you called, Pattie and I have been so nervous, we've made Myrt and Leah both suspicious."

"How is Leah?" Judd asked.

"Like I told you," Taylor said. "She's fine. Just fine."

"Fine?" Myrt walled her eyes toward the ceiling. "For a woman in her con—"

"She's going to be so surprised," Pattie said.

176 THE WANDERER

All the patrons in the establishment stood silent and still, their eyes and ears alert to Judd's every action. Hell, what was wrong? he wondered. After six months, why was he still of this much interest to the local citizens?

"Y'all have just got to see this—" The words died on Leah's lips the moment she walked out of the storeroom and saw Judd.

"Leah!" His gaze moved over her slowly, taking in every detail of the woman he'd left six months ago. Her dark hair, pulled back in a careless bun, was falling loose from its confinement. Her beautiful face was smudged with dirt. Leah held a huge box that covered her body from neck to knees, and she was holding the item as if it were made of pure gold.

"What...what are you doing here?" Leah's voice was so soft that Judd barely understood her words.

Unable to stop staring at her, soaking in the beauty of her, absorbing the pleasure of being near her again, Judd took several tentative steps in her direction. "We need to talk."

Leah glanced across the room at Pattie, who had covered her face with her hands and was peeking through her fingers. "You knew he was coming here today?"

"Yes," Pattie said, dropping her hands from her face. "Please, just listen to him. He...he's been as unhappy without you as you've been without him."

"I can vouch for that," Jared said. "Two people who care so much about each other shouldn't be apart."

Leah glanced around the shop, recognizing at least half a dozen faces. Her loyal customers seemed fascinated by the little drama unfolding before their very eyes.

Leah wondered if it was possible to turn green. Nausea, similar to what she'd known in the early months of pregnancy, overwhelmed her. She shifted the heavy box she held, clutching it tightly. She had to get out of the room before Judd realized her condition.

"Leah, you really should put down that heavy box," Myrt said. "It isn't good for you to be toting it around—"

THE WANDERER 177

"Hush," Leah said. "I'm perfectly capable of carrying a box."

"Since you Barnett brothers are in town, why don't you stay for supper?" Aunt Myrt turned to Taylor. "You see, sweetheart, I know how to play this little game."

"That's a fine idea," Jared said.

At Jared's acceptance, Myrtle Mae excused herself, asking Taylor to come along and help make preparations for their guests. With a smile on her face, Pattie began escorting customers to the door. Just as she maneuvered the last patron outside, Milly Wilson walked through the front door.

"We're closing early today, Milly," Pattie said.

"Some special reason?" Milly asked, nodding her head, motioning to the limousine parked in front of Country Class. "An out-of-town visitor?"

Ignoring everything and everyone else, Judd moved toward Leah, aware of the desperate way she held on to the huge box in her arms. "Leah, put down that ridiculous box. You're holding it as if it contained a king's ransom." When she didn't obey, he walked over to her, took the box and set it on the floor. He heard Pattie's sharp gasp, and turned to see Pattie, Jared and a pretty young woman watching him.

Trembling, Leah looked down at her feet, refusing to meet Judd's gaze when he turned around and stared at her. Judd gave her a thorough survey, from head to toe. She wore some sort of big, blue smock that was covered with grime. "What have you been doing, honey? Uncrating boxes? You always did get filthy when a new shipment came in."

With shaky fingers, Leah tried to adjust her hair and brush off her smock. Judd kept staring at her. She held her breath while he looked from her round, full breasts, straining against the material of her smock, to the large, oval swell of her protruding stomach. She saw clearly the shock in his eyes as he glanced up at her face.

"Leah?"

178   THE WANDERER

She turned, running from the shop into the storeroom. Judd ran after her. She stood, huddled against the far wall, her round, very pregnant body shaking with the force of her sobbing. Judd placed his hands on her shoulders, turning her to face him.

"Your eyes are all red and swollen, honey. You shouldn't be crying."

"What are you doing here, Judd?"

"You're pregnant."

Leah cried harder, louder. Her whole body trembled beneath his touch. He pulled her gently into his arms, depositing tender, loving kisses in her hair, on her forehead and across her closed eyelids.

She slipped her arms around his waist, snuggling her face into his chest, allowing the material of his light tan suit to absorb her tears. "I...I didn't get pregnant on purpose. We...you used precautions every time. It...it just happened."

He pushed her backward slightly, then ran his hands down her body to cup the bulge of her stomach. "Oh, Leah, why didn't you tell me?" He hadn't wanted another child, had taken every precaution to keep Leah from getting pregnant, and yet, here she was big with his baby. The very thought of another child scared him senseless. What if he failed this child the way he'd failed Steven? Dear God, did he truly deserve another chance at being a father?

Dropping to his knees in front of Leah, Judd wrapped his arms around her hips and placed his head against her belly. He gazed up at her. "You knew, didn't you, before I left Marshallton, six months ago? That's why you wouldn't agree to marry me."

"How could I marry you when you'd made it perfectly clear that—"

"I didn't want any children," he finished her sentence for her. "And you wanted my child more than you wanted me."

She reached down, grasping his face in her hands. "No, that's not true. I wanted both you and your child, but...but

THE WANDERER 179

I was so afraid...afraid you'd want me to get an abortion.''

He closed his eyes, pressing his face against her stomach, his arms nestling her closer as his hands tightened their hold. ''Do you know how scared I am? The moment I realized you were pregnant, I knew it had to be my child, and all I could think about was what if something goes wrong.''

She caressed his smooth, clean-shaved cheek with the tips of her fingers and stroked the the short, thick strands of his dark auburn hair. ''Our baby is strong and healthy. The doctor said she's perfect in every way.''

''She?'' Opening his eyes, Judd looked up at Leah. ''My daughter?'' He nuzzled Leah's belly. ''Hey there, little girl, this is your father. I guess you wonder where I've been these past few months, huh? Well...I'm here now. And I'm here to stay.'' He swallowed hard, praying that Leah was willing to give him one more chance—one last chance for happiness. ''That is, if your mother still wants me.''

When Leah tried to bend over to reach Judd, he stood up and took her into his arms, gazing at her smiling, tear-stained face. ''I've spent the past six months trying to forget you and forget how I feel about you. I've made everyone I work with hate me because I've been miserable and I've made them miserable.''

Leah ran her hand between their bodies. With great tenderness, she patted her stomach. ''At least I've had Mae Beth to keep me company. But I've missed you so much. I've cried an ocean of tears, and every time Taylor spoke to you on the phone, he'd tell me how unhappy you were. And I kept praying that you'd change your mind and...''

He felt her stiffen in his arms. ''What's wrong?''

''Did Taylor tell you that I was pregnant?'' she asked.

''I wish he had. I'd have come to my senses sooner.''

''Then you came today because...because...''

''Because I finally had the guts to admit to myself that I love you, and I can't live the rest of my life without you. I'm just sorry it took me so long to figure things out." Judd kissed the teardrops still clinging to her eyelids.

"You...you love me?"

"Yes."

"And Mae Beth? Can you love her, too?"

"I already love her," he said. "She's part of you and part of me. How could I not love her?"

Smiling, Leah choked back the fresh tears that clung in her throat. "Oh..."

"But loving her is what scares me so, Leah. The thought of losing her the way I lost Steven..." His voice grew husky. He swallowed, then cleared his throat.

"I wish that I could promise you that nothing bad will ever happen, that Mae Beth will always be safe, that—"

He covered her lips with his finger. "Shh...it's all right. I know life doesn't come with any guarantees."

Leah kissed his finger. He smiled. "I can promise you that I will always love you and stand by you no matter what happens," she said.

"And I promise you that I'll be a good father to Mae Beth. I won't ever again let Barnett, Incorporated take first place in my life. But I'm counting on you to keep me in line, and help me learn how to forgive myself for—" his voice cracked "—I know, I know. In my mind, I know it wasn't my fault, that Steven's death was an accident, but you'll have to teach my heart. The guilt's still inside me." He balled his hand into a fist, then tapped himself on the chest.

Leah grabbed his fist. Taking it in both of her hands, she spread his fingers apart and turned his palm up to her lips. She kissed his warm flesh. "Do you know how lucky we are? Some people never get the chance to find such happiness, to know a grand passion." Leah smiled, peaceful warmth flooding her, washing over her like clean, fresh rainwater over a dry, thirsty field of cotton. "You were my last chance. You know that, don't you? My first chance, my last chance, my only chance. Maybe some of us can truly

THE WANDERER 181

love only one person. I think I'm like that, and I know that you're that person."

"Is that right?" He began walking her toward the back door. She didn't hesitate to follow his lead.

"I was an old maid, willing to marry a man I didn't love. Then you walked into my life, swept me off my feet and taught me the meaning of grand passion."

Opening the back door, Judd led Leah out into the alley.

"So, I was your last chance, huh?" Ever so slowly he began to unbutton her smock.

She slapped playfully at his hand. "Stop that. You can't undress me in the middle of the street."

Lowering his head, he kissed her throat, then ran his tongue downward, into the opening he'd made at the top of her smock. "No hanky-panky in the back alley? Well, if that's the case, I guess I'll just have to marry you so I can have my way with you whenever and wherever I want."

"Marry me? When?"

Judd escorted her down the alley and out into the street. A soft, warm breeze feathered through the trees that had been strategically planted at intervals along the sidewalk. "I think the wedding should take place as soon as possible. Before Miss Mae Beth Barnett makes an untimely arrival."

"She's not due for two months. Not until mid-November."

"That should give us time for a honeymoon."

"I'm not in any condition to go on a honeymoon."

"Then we'll just lock ourselves in your room for a couple of weeks." Judd noticed that, as they made their way along the streets toward Leah's house, neighbors came outside on their front porches.

"You may not want to be locked away with me once you see what I look like without my clothes," Leah whispered, slowing her walk to a standstill. "I'm huge. Even my fingers and toes are fat."

"Such a pity," he said, shaking his head, a sad expression on his face. "Here I am, handsome, rich and power-

182   THE WANDERER

ful. I could buy myself the attentions of a dozen young, slim beauties, but I'm doomed to spend the rest of my life with..." He smiled when he noticed her staring at him, a bewildered look on her face. "With the most beautiful, desirable woman on earth. The woman I love more than life itself."

"Oh, Judd."

His sense of male possessiveness overpowered his better judgment. There, in the warm, sweet heat of a mid-September evening, on the sidewalk of Marshallton, Judd claimed the woman whose swollen body professed to the world that she was his in the most basic, elemental way a woman can belong to a man. He lifted her swiftly off her feet and into his arms, then kissed her tenderly.

Never had he imagined that he could care so deeply for another human being, to want so desperately to take care of someone. Even if life held no guarantees, he realized that he was willing to take the chance, one last chance, on loving and being loved—by his woman and their child.

"What are you doing?" Giggling, Leah slipped her arms around Judd's neck and waved at her next-door neighbors who gaped at them. "Put me down. I'm too heavy."

"You're not heavy," Judd said. "You're a little plump, but some of your weight gain has gone to the right places." He eyed her full breasts.

"You male chauvinist. Ogling me like that out here on the sidewalk where people can see." Leah laughed, her heart light and carefree and overflowing with love.

"Well, there y'all are." Myrtle Mae Derryberry stood on the sidewalk in front of Leah's two-story white house. "Bring her on in, Judd. Supper's on the table and everybody else is already here."

Epilogue

Leah leaned her head back against the wall, allowing her body to relax as she vigorously rubbed her temples. Aunt Myrt's wedding had been the most magnificent red-and-white extravaganza to ever hit the state of Tennessee. It still astonished Leah that half the population of Marshallton had shown up for the elaborately staged production. Thank goodness the Valentine's Day decorated church was still standing after enduring a live band playing hits from the fifties, a recitation by Marshallton's resident poet of Myrtle Mae's favorite Shelley poems, a procession of ten red-taffeta-attired bridesmaids, half over the age of sixty, and the release of a dozen lovebirds when Brother Brown pronounced the couple man and wife.

Just as Leah poured herself a cup of coffee and sat at the kitchen table, Judd breezed through the door humming "Here Comes the Bride."

184   THE WANDERER

"Will you please shut up." Leah laughed, turning her head slightly in order to get a good look at her handsome husband.

"Well, little Miss Mae Beth Barnett seems to have fared the big wedding better than her mother." Judd walked over to the portable crib where his fifteen-month-old, auburn-haired daughter slept peacefully.

"Do you think Hawaii is ready for Aunt Myrt?" Leah sipped her coffee, hoping the caffeine would help her throbbing head.

"Honey, our fiftieth state may secede from the union after Mr. and Mrs. Taylor spend their honeymoon on Maui."

Judd watched his slumbering child, her angelic face changing moment to moment, as if she performed her infant contortions only to amaze her father.

"I hope our house is ready to move into before the honeymooners return," Leah said. "The contractor promised us it would be finished before Valentine's Day."

"I checked with Corbinson this morning. He said next weekend at the latest, so we should be all settled in before Myrtle Mae and Taylor return and take over this place."

"Our own home." Leah sighed. "My dream house built on the site where my grandparents' home once stood."

"We could slip out the back door and drive over there to take a look. How about it?"

"I'm too tired to move, let alone go anywhere. Besides I don't think everyone's left yet, have they?" Leah asked.

"Pattie and Lisa have everything under control. So relax, Mrs. Barnett, and let your loving husband take care of you."

"What I need is to go to bed." Leah stretched, raising her arms above her head. The white organdy dress she wore rustled as she moved. "I'm probably the only matron of honor who ever wore a white dress covered in tiny red hearts."

THE WANDERER

185

"Why don't we go upstairs and I'll help you get out of your unique dress?" Judd cocked his head to one side, giving Leah's body a leering appraisal.

"Judd Barnett, you're insatiable!"

"Are you complaining?" Moving quickly, he came up behind her, reaching down to massage her bare shoulders. "This is *the* day for lovers, isn't it? I think we two lovers should make love. What do you think?"

"If that's a proposition, I'd like to take you up on it."

Judd slid his hands lower, gently covering the swell of Leah's breasts. "Are you planning on breast-feeding Mae Beth's little brother?" Judd asked.

"You know I am," she said, leaning back into his solid strength. "Just think, in six months, I'm going to give you a son." Leah leaned her head back and gazed up into Judd's dark eyes. "You aren't sorry, are you? I mean . . . that I got pregnant again so quickly...that...that this baby is a boy."

Judd squeezed her breasts tenderly as he lowered his head, his mouth nuzzling her neck. "Nothing can change the past. Nothing can bring Steven back." Strong and fierce, all the emotions swirling inside him rose to his chest. For one brief moment Judd couldn't breathe.

"Judd?"

He moved his hands downward, slowly, lovingly, until they covered her still-flat stomach. "I already love him—" Judd patted her "—as much as I do his sister."

Lifting Leah into his arms, Judd carried her out of the kitchen and down the hallway to the stairs. Pattie and Lisa, who were busy supervising the caterer's cleanup crew, smiled at Judd when he nodded toward the kitchen and mouthed the words "Watch Mae Beth."

Judd took the stairs two at a time, hurriedly making his way to their bedroom. Once inside, he laid Leah on top of the quilt covering their bed, then eased himself down on top of her.

Bracing himself on his elbows, he stared into the face of the woman he loved, the woman whose warm and gentle

186   THE WANDERER

heart had saved him from a lifetime of loneliness and despair, a lifetime of aimless wandering.

Judd covered her mouth with hard urgency. Leah's lips responded, her tongue darting out, seeking entrance. With unrelenting thrusts, Judd's own tongue delved deeply. She squirmed, pushing herself up against him. He curved his hands under her hips, lifting her against his hardness. Maneuvering her body up and down, she rubbed her soft, organdy-covered body into his arousal.

"I want you," he whispered against her neck. "Help me get you out of this damned dress."

With eager fingers, she undid the side zipper as she kicked off her satin heels. While she unclasped her strapless bra, Judd pulled the dress down her hips and threw it onto the floor. Her slip, stockings and panties followed. He watched her intently as she unbuttoned his tuxedo shirt. He flung the shirt away. She unzipped his white trousers, then slipped her hand inside his briefs to stroke him intimately.

He removed his trousers and briefs in one quick motion.

"Don't wait, Judd. I'm dying." She pulled him down, guiding him into her. When their bodies joined, she sighed with pleasure.

As he began the slow rocking rhythm of love, he sought and found her breasts. Using the tip of his tongue, he circled each pebble-hard tip. She clung to his shoulders, her nails digging into his hard flesh as the fever mounted within her, growing stronger and hotter with each plunge. He took one nipple into his mouth, sucking greedily.

Leah cried out as hot, shuddering sensations spiraled through her womanhood. "Faster," she panted. "Harder and faster."

"Now!" He thrust into her one final time, his entire body taut with desire.

"Yes, yes. Oh . . . yes." The whirlwind feeling of ecstasy claimed her, twirling her around and around as every nerve in her body exploded with shattering release.

THE WANDERER 187

Fulfillment hit him. He uttered a series of incoherent words as his big body shook with pleasure. He pulled her close. She lay in his arms, happy and content, her heart filled with happiness as her body slowly spiraled downward, relaxing, lulled by the aftermath of total satisfaction.

"Penny for your thoughts." Judd stroked her cheek with his finger, his soft gaze caressing her naked breasts.

"I'll give them to you free," she said. "I was thinking about how nice it is that Aunt Myrt and Taylor are as happy as we are."

"No one could be as happy as we are." Judd brushed his lips across her damp, swollen mouth.

"You're right... oh, Judd, I love you." She sighed, her breath mingling with his as their lips exchanged a sweet kiss.

"And I love you."

Loved and loving, Leah Marshall Barnett snuggled into her husband's arms and said a prayer of thanks. Not every woman's last chance turned out to be a dream come true.

* * * * *

COMING NEXT MONTH

CHASTITY'S PIRATE
Naomi Horton

The deal was simple. Marry pretty C.J. Carruthers and Garrett would get control of her great-aunt's company. There was just one catch—C.J. knew what was going on!

ISLAND BABY
Anne Marie Winston

Whitfield Montgomery needed a child to preserve his island home and Susannah Taylor had a baby who was going to die unless she had surgery. Could they help each other?

HER KIND OF MAN
Barbara McCauley

Rachel Stephens had to remarry to regain control of her ranch, but Cord Cantrell turned her down flat—until he heard her propose to the next man on her list!

COMING NEXT MONTH

FOUND FATHER
Justine Davis

Devlin Cross had left Megan Spencer without a word because he didn't have any words to excuse or explain what he had done. Now, years later, Megan didn't want to listen to why Dev had left her and her unborn son!

THURSDAY'S CHILD
Kat Adams

When Marlie Stynhearst discovered that her orphaned nephew wasn't really her nephew at all, she decided she had to find the child's real parents. Widower Bryce Powell suddenly had the power to break her heart...

TENNESSEE WALTZ
Jackie Merritt

Clover Dove didn't want to fall for a talented entertainer like her parents. She wanted a normal life, but the only man who interested her was Will Lang and he was *very* special and *very* talented...

MYSTERY DATES!

Six sexy bachelors explosively pair with six sultry sirens to find the love of a lifetime.

Get to know the mysterious men who breeze into the lives of these unsuspecting women. Slowly uncover—as the heroines themselves must do—the missing pieces of the puzzle that add up to hot, *hot* heroes! You begin by knowing nothing about these enigmatic men, but soon you'll know *everything*...

Heat up your summer with:

THE COWBOY by Cait London
THE STRANGER by Ryanne Corey
THE RESCUER by Peggy Moreland
THE WANDERER by Beverly Barton
THE COP by Karen Leabo
THE BACHELOR by Raye Morgan

Mystery Dates—coming in July from Silhouette Desire. You never know who you'll meet...

COMING NEXT MONTH FROM

Silhouette

Sensation

*romance with a special mix of
suspense, glamour and drama*

NOT WITHOUT HONOUR Marilyn Pappano
FOREVER MY LOVE Heather Graham Pozzessere
SIR FLYNN AND LADY CONSTANCE Maura Seger
LOVING LIES Ann Williams

Special Edition

*longer, satisfying romances with
mature heroines and lots of emotion*

TRUE BLUE HEARTS Curtiss Ann Matlock
HARDWORKING MAN Gina Ferris
YOUR CHILD, MY CHILD Jennifer Mikels
LIVE, LAUGH, LOVE Ada Steward
MAN OF THE FAMILY Andrea Edwards
FALLING FOR RACHEL Nora Roberts

SUMMER Sizzlers

Red-hot romance!

Three sizzling short stories from top Silhouette authors, bound into one volume.

Silhouette

Available July 1993   Price: £3.99

Available from W.H. Smith, John Menzies, Martins, Forbuoys, most supermarkets and other paperback stockists. Also available from Mills & Boon Reader Service, FREEPOST, PO Box 236, Thornton Road, Croydon, Surrey CR9 9EL. (UK Postage & Packaging free)